Tomorrow's Roses

Bernadette Piper

 A catalogue record for this book is available from the National Library of Australia

Linellen Press
265 Boomerang Road
Oldbury, Western Australia
www.linellenpress.com.au

Dedication

To Mum, Dad, and Aunty Nancy.

Contents

Acknowledgments

Thank you, Betty O'Mara for the beautiful internal artwork you produced for this book.

Many thanks to Helen Iles for all her editing and suggestions, and help bringing this book to life.

Prologue

April 1945

The sounds of laughter and chatter ceased as women fled, their gardening and gossiping over fences interrupted. Young children were hurried inside. Curtains moved; eyes peered out of windows. Seagulls squawked in the blue sky, and the whistles of boats floated on the warm autumn breeze. The bicycle turned into Solomon Street.

Kate Kelly looked up from her gardening, rose and stretched her back, and shaded her eyes. She did not hurry inside – there was no need for her to do that.

The bicycle stopped at her gate. That was wrong.

Kate laid her gardening tool on the ground, wiped dirt from her knees and clapped her shaking hand together. Straightening, she looked ahead … hesitated. There was no choice: she had to walk down that pathway.

Kate opened the gate, stepped through it and pulled it shut behind her, clutching the latch as she looked the boy in the eyes.

He turned his face away; looked across the road to the house opposite.

'I'm sorry, Mrs Kelly,' he said.

'It's not your fault,' Kate said. 'Would you like me to take it for you?'

'No,' he said. 'It's my responsibility.'

The boy crossed the road, leant his bicycle on the front fence, opened the gate, and walked down the path; He climbed the few steps and knocked on the door. Peg Kennedy opened the door. He put the telegram in her trembling hands, turned and walked away. There was nothing else to do.

The boy gave Kate a sad smile as he passed her on his way to another delivery.

Kate dragged her fingers from her gate and wiped her cheeks with the back of her hand. She stumbled as she crossed the road, but walked staunchly down the path, up the steps and opened the door. Peg stood in the hallway, the telegram in her hand, tears streaming down her face. She handed the paper to Kate. There was no need to read the words; she knew what they said before her eyes recognised them. *Missing in action, presumed dead.*

'It can't be! Not now! Not after all this time,' Peg said. Her hands knotted together as she paced the hallway. Kate reached out to comfort her, but Peg pushed her away.

'Not now! Not my Billy!'

'Peg …'

'He can't be dead. Wouldn't I feel something? Wouldn't I know in my heart? Did you know?' she asked Kate.

Kate couldn't answer that question. What could she say? All the usual, stupid words … we have the children … we have to carry on … the pain dulls – words that were of no comfort to her then and would be no comfort to her ever again.

Peg pulled the telegram from Kate and shook her head. Then she said, 'I'm going to make a cup of tea. Do you want a cup of tea?'

Kate was alone in the hallway. Had she known when Patrick died? It seemed so long ago. Would she know now? Her hand on the wall kept her upright.

Crockery crashed and shattered the quiet, and Kate hurried into the kitchen. The telegram on the wooden table glared at her. Smashed china covered the floor; Peg stood staring at it.

'I dropped it.'

She backed away from the broken china, knocked over a chair and trapped herself against the wall. Her legs buckled, and she slid to the floor. Kate took her in her arms and rocked her like a baby.

There is nothing to say … no words that will help.

Patrick … they had argued.

'Why,' she'd said. 'Why do you have to go?'

He'd shrugged his shoulders and gave her his, *it's-what-I-have-to-do* look.

'You don't believe in the Great British Empire. It's not what's important to you. You don't owe them anything!' Kate had said.

It was the end of 1939.

'Billy's going,' Patrick had replied. 'I have to look after him.'

Kate knew then she'd lost the argument. Nevertheless, she said, 'But who will look after you?'

'We will look after each other. I promise I'll be careful.'

You don't know how to be careful.

'Don't worry,' he'd said. 'It's an adventure – boys together – overseas – somewhere we'd never get to go. We'll be all right. We'll be home soon.'

But he hadn't been home soon, and her anger and despair might have destroyed her. She was a sensible girl, though, and she had her baby and, like many others, she had pulled her life back together.

Could she do that again?

Tears fell as she held her sobbing friend, another name tearing at her heart.

Chapter One

Fremantle, Western Australia
December 1944.

'Mummy,' Kate's daughter murmured as she reached out and slipped her hand into her grandmother's.

'It's all right, Jessie,' Kate said. *Could it be all right?*

Kate stood on the corner of Solomon Street and Fothergill Road, the sun still low in the blue sky – if you wanted to catch fish, you had to get up early.

'Harry, hold Sam,' she told the little boy with her.

Kate glanced at her mother-in-law. Mary's face was pale, her eyes staring. She pulled Jessie close.

A black car had parked down the road, in front of Kate's home, and three men in uniform were alighting from the vehicle.

Men in uniform weren't unusual – Fremantle, where they lived, was full of men and women in uniform; it was a Naval base for the Australian Navy and their Allies. Warships and merchant ships used the harbour, and a Submarine Base was out near the South Mole. The town centre was a hive of wartime activity, the hotels were full, a black market operated, and some girls earnt money as prostitutes. None of this concerned Kate and her family, but this black car parked at her front gate did.

Sam barked, and the men now standing beside the car looked up the street. It was then Kate noticed the flag on the car bonnet, the Stars and Stripes blowing in the warm wind.

Two of the men, in white uniforms, were tall and carried their hats under one arm. The third man was in khaki, an Australian Army khaki uniform. The third man was Frank Kelly.

Kate wanted to run down the road and throw her arms around

him, hold him tight, never let him go, but she didn't do that – he was Mary's son.

Mary trundled down the road faster. When Frank saw her, he rushed to meet her. She rested her head on his chest as he folded her in his arms.

Kate continued to walk down the road, keeping the children together. The dog beside her growled, and she patted his head to reassure him.

Then, at last, *she* was in Frank's arms; they held each other tight, tighter than they should; more tightly than they were allowed, but he was home. She pushed him away, to look, to make sure he wasn't injured.

'I'm in one piece,' he said.

'How?' Kate asked.

He hadn't been home for over two years; they hadn't expected to see him, and he hadn't said anything in his last letter.

'Been ordered home for some leave … got a ride with these fellas.' He indicated the two men standing down the road next to the black sedan.

He reached out to her little girl. 'This is Jessie! My, she has grown.'

Jessie backed away from his touch.

'Jessie, this is Uncle Frank,' Kate said.

Frank turned to the boy and said, 'You must be …?'

'Harry,' the boy said.

'Ahh, Harry Kennedy?' Frank said. 'I'm Father Kelly.'

He extended his hand to the boy, and Harry shook it, then he ran down the road, calling, 'Mum, Mum, we got some fish.'

***

Michael Brannigan stood beside a black car. A little boy with dark curly hair raced by shouting to his mother. Frank Kelly had sprinted up the road to meet his family; he'd held his mother in his arms, while the younger woman stood back. Then Frank drew her into his arms.

Frank walked down the road with his arm around his mother. The younger woman held the little girl by the hand and walked close to Frank. She would reach out and touch him on the arm every now and then.

Frank's family. His *family*! Michael took a breath and shook his head.

The little girl scurried past the car, her head down; she opened the gate and hurried down the pathway. The younger woman placed the canvas bag she carried on the ground, crouching she called the agitated dog to her and said, 'Go with Jessie, boy.'

The dog waddled through the gate; turned once to look at her then padded down the path to sit on the front step by the little girl's feet.

When the younger woman stood up, her eyes met his. He helped her up, and she stood before him staring into his eyes. His heart lurched – he hadn't expected that.

***

Kate stared into brown eyes, into eyes that could overwhelm her. She released the hand that had helped her up and pushed her hair away from her face. How untidy she was. The shorts she wore were still damp from standing in the river, her father's old khaki jumper was tatty and full of holes. Even though she'd washed her hands with sand and river water, she rubbed them on the back of her shorts when Frank introduced her and Mary to the men beside the car.

Joseph Daniels was the Captain of the United States Submarine Codfish. His blue eyes sparkled in a clean-shaven face; the wind ruffled his blond hair. Kate returned his smile with ease. He squeezed her fingers when he shook her hand and it was like she had known him all her life.

The other man was his second-in-command, Lieutenant Commander Michael Brannigan. He was also clean-shaven, taller than his Captain, and more solid, his dark curls too short for the breeze to disturb. Lines were forming under his brown eyes, eyes that had caught Kate off guard.

Kate shook Michael's hand, the touch of his fingers sending a shiver up her arm, again. Her fingers trembled; her heart pounded. She knew she should remove her hand from his, but didn't, his hand fitting around hers like it should be there.

***

Michael held Kate's hand, her fingers trembling in his palm. Strands of her dark hair escaped from the braid that sat between her shoulders and blew across her face. He wanted to reach out, take the hair in his fingers, push it out of her blue eyes, eyes that locked with his, eyes that made him vulnerable and exposed.

He knew he should look away, remove his hand, but did neither. He wondered why he could feel his heart beating; why he wanted to hold her body close to his, to kiss her lips, to be part of someone.

This wasn't right: he wasn't going to open that part of his life – it was over, locked away out of harm's way. He removed his hand and pulled himself back under control.

***

Kate turned away from Michael, bewildered. Joseph Daniels was no threat, so she said to him, 'We have caught fish and are going to have breakfast. Would you care to join us?'

'I'm sorry, we can't stay,' Joe said. 'We have to be elsewhere. We are just bringing Frank home to you.'

Smiling, he looked at Michael and said, 'Some other time though.'

'Frank Kelly, it is you!' Peg Kennedy called. She ran down the pathway of the house opposite, Harry following her.

'Yes, Peg,' Frank said.

He kissed her on the cheek and introduced her to Joe and Michael. It was time for the men to leave, the car attracting attention from those who were up early on the street.

Kate, chewing her fingernails, watched the car turned out of Solomon Street. She could still feel Michael's fingers in her hand. She shook her head; she couldn't do that, not here, not now, not with him. It wasn't safe. She had made a promise she could not break – she had her girls to look after, had to do that, wanted to do that.

Kate heard her daughter say, 'Come on, Mummy … we're hungry.'

Mummy, who feeds hungry children, that was who she was. That was safe.

Kate opened the gate and walked down the path to join her family, to eat and share the news.

Chapter Two

On the 16th of December 1944, Jean Stanford, munition's worker and grocer's daughter married Nick James, a seaman from the United States Submarine Codfish. The bride wore silk and lace. The groom was in uniform. Father Francis Kelly performed the ceremony at St Patrick's Catholic Church on Adelaide Street.

A celebration for the young couple took place in the church hall which had been decorated by family and friends. The local ladies supplied food for the buffet; the groom's shipmates provided the alcohol.

***

Kate Kelly and her family were guests at the wedding. The bride had called on her in September seeking her advice. She told Kate she had met a sailor, how she loved him, and how hard it was to say no to him, telling Kate he wanted to marry her. They laughed, and Kate said they should hurry up and get married.

In November, Jean told her the wedding was to be before Christmas. There was no money or material to make a proper wedding dress. She said Nick's mother lived somewhere called Virginia. The ladies in their town were arranging wedding dresses for Australian girls marrying 'their boys'. It was a kind idea, but she didn't want to wear one of those.

Kate took her into her bedroom and removed a cardboard box from the top shelf of her cupboard. It contained a dress of white silk and lace, which was a little out of date. She had copied the style from a dress Ginger Rodgers wore in a movie. It had short sleeves and buttons down the front, a silk ribbon tied around the waist, and the long flowing skirt had three rows of silk ribbon around the hem. Kate might still squeeze into the 24-inch waist, but she would never wear it again. So there was no reason to keep it. Jean could have it, even if she only used the fabric.

The bride was radiant in her wedding dress. She had changed it and added some extra ribbon to make it memorable for her.

Kate sat with her parents, Sean and Kathleen O'Brien, her sister Ruth, home on leave from the army for her best friend's wedding, her daughter Jessie, and niece Tilly. Frank and Mary Kelly also shared their table.

Kate wasn't focused on the bride and groom. She'd noticed Michael Brannigan and Joseph Daniels sitting at a crowded table across the hot, noisy, room. She wondered … why had she acted the way she had when she met Michael? She was a grown woman, a sensible grown woman. The way her heart had raced and how her body had responded to his touch had alarmed her. She hadn't expected to see him again and thought she had put him out of her mind. She was wrong.

***

Michael Brannigan was having trouble keeping his mind in one place. The way he'd reacted when he met Kate, his heart speeding up, the sensation of her hand in his, he didn't think he still had those feelings; he didn't want them; he didn't want the pain they caused. He hadn't expected to see her again and had tried to put her out of his mind. He was not succeeding.

And now here he was, sitting at a crowded table on a hot December day as one of his crew celebrated his marriage to a local girl. Nick James had asked his permission to marry and had begged: 'Please don't make us wait six months. She's a good girl, and we might do something we might regret.'

The officers of a naval vessel didn't usually socialise with their crew. On a submarine, where officers are known to get oil on their hands, it was different. Joseph Daniels had given permission for this marriage to take place – it would be impolite to refuse an invitation to the wedding.

Michael tried to keep his mind on the conversation around him.

He talked to women he didn't know and did not need to know, as he watched the one, who might make him take a chance, leave her table.

***

Kate stood on the porch with her parents and Frank and Mary Kelly. The mid-afternoon sun burnt skin and sapped energy. They moved into the shade of a big eucalyptus tree.

'I won't be long. Tilly wants to stay and dance,' Kate said. It was nice to see Tilly enjoying herself. She'd be fifteen next year, and her young life was full of turmoil. Listening to music and dancing would be good for her, but only under proper supervision.

Kate kissed her daughter on the top of her head and said, 'Be good for Nannie and Pop.'

'She always is,' Kathleen O'Brien said as she took her granddaughter's hand.

Sean O'Brien offered his arm to Mary Kelly.

Kate and Frank stood in the shade and watched their families walk down the pathway and out onto the street. Inside, the band began to play.

'Well, Mrs Kelly, would you care to dance?' Frank asked.

He was out of his priest's robes and back in khaki. His uniform hung on his body, and his five-foot ten-inch height seemed stunted.

Inside the hall filled with smoke, people mingled. Tables and chairs moved, dancers changed partners. Family and friends invited visitors into their groups. Parents watched over their daughters.

Kate assured herself Tilly would come to no harm and enjoyed dancing with her dear friend. Eventually, Frank returned Kate to her table and excused himself as he had many people to speak to.

Watching the dancers, Kate tried not to think of the man in the white uniform on the other side of the hall. At the table he shared with others, they had company. Tilly and Ruth returned and slid onto the chairs beside her, and she turned her attention to them. But she was soon alone again. So, when a hand stretched down to invite her to dance, she accepted and joined a burly red-haired man as the band played an old Irish ballad. One, two, three, four, to eight forwards, one, two, three, four, to eight back – an old dance learnt long ago at school. His name was Jack Morgan, the 'Chief' of the boat.

The Pride of Erin concluded, and the band announced a change of pace. Kate excused herself, unsure of the new modern step, and Jack Morgan returned to her table. She sat alone, humming and tapping her toes to the music when a young sailor asked her to dance. She shook her head, saying she didn't know the steps; he said it was easy, and he would show her. She took his arm, and they entered the crowded dance floor. He seemed so young. He was very confident of his dancing abilities, and she was soon dancing the steps he showed her. After a couple of dances, Kate was warm and breathless, and he returned her to her table.

'Thank you, ma'am,' he said.

Ma'am? Isn't that what you called an old lady? She didn't feel that old, but said, 'I'm getting too old for this.'

'Never,' he said gallantly. He noticed the pretty red-haired girl seated at the table.

'May I have this dance?' he asked.

Tilly looked at Kate for approval, and she shooed them onto the dance floor and closed her eyes.

She did feel too old to be doing the 'bug', as he called it; she was out of breath and leant back on her chair. *Too old,* she thought. *Thirty-two next year.*

Was it so long ago? Sometimes it felt like another life. Patrick loved to dance and sing. They would dance on Saturdays, when they could, then he had gone to war, and she hadn't danced since. Kate opened her eyes. Smoke was drifting out the open windows, pushed by the salt-laden air that blew in off the ocean. Michael Brannigan stood in front her, his hand held out. He said, 'May I have this dance?'

***

Michael had danced with several of the ladies present. He had spent time talking with them at their tables. It was his duty as second in command. He'd watched Kate dancing with 'Chief' Morgan, and having fun with young Emerson. He had done his duty. Now he wanted to dance with her.

She wore a blue floral halter dress and had a navy jacket hung over the back of the chair. Her dark wavy hair was tied at the nape of her neck in a pale blue ribbon, the ribbon slipping and leaving strands falling loose. He twined those strands through his fingers and pushed them from her face. She took his hand.

They danced, keeping a proper distance between them. And they talked … about the wedding, about the weather, about nothing. He ran his fingers through the loose strands of her hair again, her response revealing he could hold her tighter.

It was hot on the dance floor, the cooling breeze having little effect, and many dancers left the floor to find relief. Michael and Kate danced on, unaware of the interest they attracted.

Then the band concluded their set and took a break.

***

Kate knew her cheeks were pink; she could feel the heat in them when Michael took her to the table he sat at and introduced her to his friends. She was pleased to see Joseph Daniels among the men who stood as she arrived.

Frank Kelly joined the group shortly after, bringing with him his dancing partner, Ethel Ingram. Kate knew Ethel from her Red Cross duties and church. Ethel's husband's posting in Malaya had been overrun by the Japanese, and he was now a prisoner of war. Like many other women, she was keeping busy. As they sat chatting, Ethel asked after everyone's homes and families.

Families!

Kate glanced at the man she had danced with – she'd not considered he could be married. She should have been more careful. Why hadn't she been more careful?

She heard Joseph Daniels say, 'I have two boys.'

'And you, Lieutenant? Do you have any children?' Ethel asked.

'I have a daughter,' Michael answered. He looked away from Kate, then excused himself and left the table.

Confused, Kate watched him leave. How could she have been so wrong! Of course he has a family … a daughter and wife, and he must miss them. She had let herself down; she had let herself get swept away by his touch, by what her heart was telling her she might want. They should not have been dancing like that, and she should be angry with him, and with herself for doing so.

The band began to play a Bing Crosby Christmas ballad. Many homesick sailors, young and older, began to show the effects of loneliness, alcohol, and the heat. Dancing resumed but at a more sedate pace.

It was time for Kate to leave; she'd been reckless. Michael was a married man. How could she have been so stupid? She should have been sensible, kept her heart locked away. Surely, he would not hold her like that if he wasn't free to do so? But he has a daughter and a wife somewhere. She shouldn't have let herself down. But it had been a long time … maybe she was lonely.

Frank offered to see her home, so she found Tilly and told her they were leaving.

'But Ruth is staying on, why can't I?' Tilly protested.

'Because Ruth is older and responsible for herself. I am responsible for you, so you need to come home now. I will meet you on the front steps in five minutes.' She shook her head – it wasn't always easy bringing up a fourteen-year-old girl, and she didn't want to fight tonight.

Kate waited impatiently on the veranda for Tilly to join her, the late afternoon sun still warm, the shade from the gum tree now having fled. Tilly came out of the hall, accompanied by a young man.

'May I walk Tilly home?' Tommy Ingram asked.

'Yes, of course,' Kate replied.

The young couple walked down the pathway past a solitary figure sitting on a bench under the tree.

'Ready,' Frank Kelly said as he came out the hall door. He took her arm, and they walked down the three steps onto the cement pathway.

***

Michael Brannigan watched the young couple as they hurried by him then became aware Kate and Frank Kelly had stopped where he sat. He rose from the seat, his hat in his hands, his eyes squinting in the sun; unsure. How could he have been so wrong about Kate? *She must be married …* her reaction when the conversation turned to families. He hadn't thought about that: her husband must be away at war. But when they had danced together it had felt so right holding her in his arms. Maybe she was lonely; maybe he was lonely. *Maybe it's better this way.* He certainly didn't want to risk that pain again. He was a coward.

From the step of the veranda, Ethel Ingram called, 'Father Kelly, Father Kelly? Are you busy?'

'I'll be all right,' Kate said to Frank. 'I must go after Tilly. You see to Ethel.'

'May I walk you home?' Michael asked.

***

Kate should not let him do that – the sensible girl knew that. The rules she'd put in place for herself, the rules she grew up with … Everything told her she could not.

But she had danced with him.

'Please do,' she said.

'I will see you tomorrow,' Frank Kelly said.

He hugged Kate then offered his hand to Michael. Kate caught the look in Frank's eye: what was he trying to tell her? She glanced back as she opened the church gate; saw Frank watching her and Michael. Then he turned to Ethel.

Chapter Three

Kate walked briskly and caught up with Tilly and Tommy.

'Mrs Kelly, I'm going to enlist,' Tommy said. 'I'll be eighteen soon then I can join up. I hope I get to do some fighting.'

'Oh,' Kate said. Tommy was nearly eighteen; how quickly that had happened.

The walk took them through the Port town, up the High Street, past the prison with its thick walls and lookout towers. The town was preparing for the night as the late afternoon sun waned and sent long shadows across the land. Inside, lights were being turned on behind blackout curtains; outside there was still a little light left in the day. When it was dark, the streetlights would turn on under browned out lamps.

***

Michael noticed Kate stiffen as she heard those words. He had done 'some fighting', and this young man didn't understand what it all meant, but he would soon find out. He placed his hand on Kate's arm but, when she looked into his eyes, he removed it. They followed the young couple in silence until he asked: 'How old is your daughter?'

'Six,' Kate said.

'Six?' The girl in front of him was older than that.

'Oh no, Tilly is my niece, my brother's child,' she said, smiling slightly. 'After his wife died, he took Tilly to Malaya to start a new life, but the war ruined that. Robert was able to get Tilly on a ship leaving Singapore, but he stayed behind to do some business. We've heard nothing from him since.'

The barriers Michael had set up were ripping to pieces.

He asked her more about herself.

She told him her life was ordinary. Coming from Ireland as a baby, going to school, growing up in this small seaside town. She'd worked in a haberdashery shop, got married, had Jessie, all very ordinary. She was one of four children; had a brother and two sisters.

He had to know, so he asked, 'Your husband?'

Kate stopped walking and faced him. She chewed her bottom lip before saying, 'He was killed in Africa four years ago.'

'I'm sorry,' he said.

'Yes.'

And he was sorry; he wanted to put his arms around her, hold her tight, but that wouldn't be right. Not yet.

They continued walking through the darkening township.

***

Kate stopped at a white picket fence and said, 'I have to pick up my daughter.' She opened the gate, walked down the path onto the veranda, and opened the front door. Her father shook the hand Michael offered and showed him into the front room where Kate's mother sat with Jessie curled up beside her.

'Come on, sleepyhead. Time to go,' Kate said as she lifted her child from the settee. Jessie grizzled, not wanting to walk.

'It's not far … come on now.'

'No.' She flopped back onto the settee beside her grandmother.

'All right, all right.' *Why does everyone want to argue today?* Kate thought as she bent to lift her daughter.

'Please let me?' Michael said.

'I can manage,' Kate snapped.

She was annoyed, with herself, and him. His body was too close; she should not have let him walk her home. Why had he asked her? A married man.

Kate knew what was expected of her, knew what was allowed, knew what she expected of herself.

'I know,' he said.

Yet she stepped away from the chair and allowed him to pick up her child.

'Mummy!'

'Shush, shush,' Michael said. He patted Jessie on the back.

'It's all right. Go back to sleep,' Kate said, caressing her child's cheek.

Jessie closed her eyes again and lay her head on Michael's shoulder. He carried her out onto the front veranda.

'See you tomorrow,' Kate said to her parents.

Kate opened the front gate into her own garden and walked down the pathway; climbed the two steps onto the veranda. The old dog at the front door growled at the unfamiliar figure, and Kate patted his head.

'It's all right, boy.'

His duty done, the dog walked around the side of the house to the back veranda.

Kate unlocked the front door and showed Michael to the second bedroom down the hallway. Then she went through the house and opened windows to let out the heat of the day; she closed the blackout curtains and turned on the lights in the kitchen. Unlatching the back door for Tilly, she made sure the young man with her was saying his goodbyes and leaving.

Kate returned to the bedroom and stood at the doorway, watching as Michael lay Jessie on the bed. The little girl stirred as her light brown curls fell across her face. He pushed them aside. 'Goodnight, little one,' he whispered. Kate's heart broke for him, his daughter so far away.

Her resolve embedded in her – she could not let this happen, not with a married man, not with any man. Not while the war was on and maybe never. She didn't think she could survive the pain of separation and loss again. And she barely knew him.

Michael was a married man. She could not do that.

Kate joined him at the bedside, but he turned and left the room. She removed her child's clothing – Jessie could sleep in her underwear, it was too hot for nightclothes – too hot for heavy bedding, so she pulled a sheet up over her sleeping child. When Kate kissed Jessie's cheek, the tears in her eyes spilled over.

'Kate?' Tilly queried from the bedroom door.

Kate wiped her eyes, turned to her niece, and said, 'The Lieutenant carried Jessie home for me. She's getting heavy now.'

'Kate?' Tilly queried.

'What is it, Tilly?'

'Tommy asked me to go to the dance with him tomorrow night. It's at the church hall, and Father Kelly will be there.'

Father Kelly, Kate smiled: that would make a difference.

'That would be nice. Tell Tommy at Mass tomorrow morning you can go.'

'Thank you.' Then the girl hesitated. 'Do you think the war will end soon? I wish and pray every night it will. I hope my daddy's safe.'

Kate folded the young woman in her arms, and they sat together on the other bed in the room.

'Be brave, you know daddy would want that. Remember how big and strong he is. Nothing could ever hurt him. Now go and get ready for bed.'

It was becoming harder to keep the pretence up as Tilly grew older. That list of dead and missing was there every day in the paper, not so long now, but still there.

Her father must be alive.

Michael Brannigan was someone's father.

The western horizon glowed orange and yellow. Michael sat on the top step overlooking the back garden and the setting sun. The wire door creaked when Kate opened it, and he turned to stand.

'Don't get up,' she said and sat beside him.

Her pet lifted his head from Michael's knee and sought her attention. She ran her fingers through the fur around his ears.

'He likes you,' she said

'I'm afraid I startled your niece,' Michael said.

'That's all right. The girls are not used to having strangers around.' She should have said the girls are not used to having men around.

The warm wind blew across the darkening land and out to sea. Trees moaned, and leaves flew wildly around the dry ground.

'It will be hot tomorrow,' Kate said.

She turned to wish her niece goodnight as Tilly returned from the bathroom.

Patrick had moved the bathroom from the backyard when he had repaired the house. How excited he'd been about restoring the house. It was falling to pieces, the windows were broken, the building sloping down the block, but it was cheap, and he could fix it up … they could have their own home. *Will you marry me?*

She'd insisted on contributing her savings, and while he wasn't happy about that, she'd had her way. How lucky she'd been, having Patrick as her husband.

And Michael was someone's husband. She shouldn't have let him walk her home.

'My daughter will be ten on her next birthday,' he said. 'I haven't seen her for three years. I don't think she will even remember me.'

'Yes, she will.' Kate surprised herself. How calm her voice had sounded. 'The war will end one day, and then you will go home to your wife and daughter.'

'I lost my wife and son in an automobile accident,' he said.

Kate took his hands. The last light of day showed the rawness of grief in his eyes, but his trembling hands held hers tight. Then he turned his left wrist, glanced at the Rolex there, and said, 'I have to go.'

He picked his hat up, rose from the step and helped her up. The last of the daylight was behind her as she looked up into his face. He wiped the dampness from her cheeks with his fingers, then patted the old dog on the head. There were no words she could say.

It was better not to try. The dog made his way to his blanket near the back door.

When Kate opened the front door to see him out, wind rushed through the house, down the hallway into the kitchen, and slammed the back door. They stood together on the front veranda, her hair tangling around her face, and she gathered the loose strands in her hand. Michael stood with his hat in his.

'I would like to see you again,' he said.

Kate wasn't sure. If she hadn't been in his arms … If he hadn't run his fingers through her hair … If she hadn't held his trembling hands … maybe it would have been easy to say no.

'I would like that,' she said.

'Tomorrow?'

'My family are going to South Beach tomorrow – we will be there most of the day. I will be home in the evening.'

He put his hat on, and took her hands as he said, 'I will see you tomorrow.'

Then he strode down the pathway onto the darkening street. Kate stood on the front veranda and watched him walk away.

Chapter Four

The next day, the sun blazed down through a blue sky that sizzled; grass and plants shrivelled. The tram ride along South Terrace was hot and uncomfortable.

Kate and the girls soon walked with Peg, Harry and Mary across the grassed esplanade, past the wooden pavilion to the white sand where umbrellas dotted the beach and small waves fell on the shore. People crowded the shallow water; the more adventurous and stronger swimmers were out deeper.

Where the grass met the sand, rows of old and slightly crumbling beach shelters stood. These provided some protection for the few early enough to secure one. Kate found her parents in one of these shelters.

The children, rushing their hellos and dropping their belongings, ran across the hot sand, squealing and jumping until they reached the cooling water.

Kate removed her outer clothing and tidied up the mess, felt the hot sun burning her skin as she talked with her parents. She joined the children at the water's edge and kicked water around her ankles, thinking.

She loved Patrick Kelly; they had known each other so long and so well; he had always been in her life. But he had gone to war and taken her love and life with him. She wasn't going to love someone who could do that to her again and had therefore created a secure world for herself and the girls. The walls of that world were being pushed down.

'Penny for them?'

She turned to face her father, Sean O'Brien. His face showed his age, but his dark brown eyes revealed he knew everything that went on.

'I was miles away,' Kate replied

'Miles?'

'Not here, anyway.'

Her father said, 'Kate, this American sailor … he obviously has children. Is he married?' Her father always spoke directly with her. It was one of his endearing qualities.

'Oh, Dad, he has a daughter, but his wife and son died in an automobile accident.'

He took her hands.

'Anyway, you know me. Have I ever done anything I shouldn't?'

'No, you haven't, but then I've never seen you like this either. You have always been my most sensible girl, always known your mind.'

'That's right. I'm the sensible one. I think I'll have a swim. The girls should be all right.'

'I'll keep an eye on them,' he said.

Kate splashed water up her legs and onto her swimsuit as she walked into the water. When it was deep enough, she swam out into the ocean until she ran out of breath. Then she floated on her back and let the sun warm her face.

The ocean gave her so much — the white sands, the clean blue water, the smell of salt and seaweed in the air. She found joy and peace in the sun and the sea. Even in the winter, when the storms would blow, there was so much beauty and strength to find. She could think clearly, make her decisions. Today was different.

She swam back to the sandy beach. Jessie and Tilly, who wasn't too old to make sandcastles today, sat above the waterline. Incoming waves bought water into the moat around their sandcastle. Kate watched the water fill the moat till the edges fell in.

The quiet was shattered by the arrival of three noisy, boisterous children, Kate's two fair-haired, freckle-faced nephews aged twelve and ten, and her dark-haired, freckle-faced niece, aged seven. The children ran across the grass, shouting greetings to their grandparents. They tossed their clothing on the ground and ran into the water. Their father followed them crashing onto the water and swimming out deep. The children followed until the littlest could barely stand. Her mother shouted from the shore to take care of them. Their father returned to his children, lifted the littlest one onto his shoulders and watched his boys at play.

George Jefferies was a big man. Tall and sturdy, he had blond hair, receding at the temples, blue eyes, and his skin was covered in freckles. Kate joined him in the shallow water, and he greeted her as he always did, with a peck on the cheek. He worked at the Midland Railway Workshop and was man-powered out of the war – not allowed to enlist. The family's relief at this was not shared by George. As time went by, and friends and family members did not return from the war, he began to understand.

A call came from the beach shelter – it was time to eat. Kate kissed her sister in greeting.

Iris was four years older than Kate. Her auburn hair sat on her collar, and she had her father's dark brown eyes. She was a little thicker around the waist than she wanted to be and a bit taller than Kate. She had the same small nose and rounded chin, definitely sisters to those who saw them together.

The families had met at this spot in December 1939 before Billy and Patrick had gone away to war. *They would be back by next Christmas,* and the families would meet once again at this spot.

But Patrick and Billy were not back by the next Christmas; they were on their way to Africa to fight.

Patrick would never return. But the families continued to meet each other every year, hoping that one day it would be the last Christmas apart.

Food was shared and enjoyed, each family supplying something for the picnic. Fruit and vegetables were grown in season. Chickens were kept for eggs, and meat, if anyone had the heart to kill them. Rabbits could be caught if you had the skill.

The cooling breeze was so gentle as it came in over the ocean, it did not shift the sand, and it was still pleasant on the beach. The children fed, a game of cricket was set up. Their mothers cleared away the remains of the meal, tidied up all the tossed towels, then sat and watched the game.

Kate left her daughter in the care of her grandmothers and went for a walk.

'Aunty Kate, Aunty Kate.' She heard the words on the breeze. Her sister's eldest boy, Edward, ran after her. 'Aunty Kate,' he puffed as he caught up to her. 'Father Kelly's here.'

Kate looked back to where her family sat. Frank was not alone. Joseph Daniels and Michael Brannigan were with him. So, what did that mean? She hurried to return with her nephew.

'The Codfish has been ordered back to sea, and I have to go with her,' Frank Kelly was saying.

Kate saw him take his mother's hand – her own heartbreak would be nothing compared to Mary's. She sat on the bench beside her father.

The cricket game came to a halt, the children becoming restless. An offer of ice-cream from the pavilion sent them running in that direction.

'Would you care to join us?' Sean O'Brien addressed Joe Daniels.

'I'm afraid we cannot,' Joe said. 'We needed to see Frank and are heading back to the dock.'

Frank turned to Joe. 'Thank you for the lift. I'll be ready when you leave.' He shook the hands offered.

Joe and Michael turned to leave.

Kate surprised herself by asking, 'May I join you?'

Michael took her hand and helped her from the seat, released it as soon as she was standing; she walked with Joe and Michael across the grassed esplanade. The black car was parked in front of an old hotel. She would say goodbye from here, in private away from her families' eyes. It was safer, him leaving now.

Joseph Daniels said, 'I can manage without you for a few hours, Mike. Why don't you stay.'

Then he took Kate's hands and said, 'Goodbye, I will see you again.'

Kate held Joe's hand tight and kissed his cheek, 'Goodbye, Joe … see you again.'

Kate and Michael stood on the shore. The gentle breeze had turned into a strong gusty wind that now picked up sand and tossed it about. The heat had gone out of the day, and the beach became deserted as beachgoers packed their belongings.

'Shall we walk?' Kate suggested. Her homemade one-piece cotton swimsuit was almost dry, but her white calico shorts were still wet. Nevertheless, she splashed in the water. In a pool left by a receding wave, a tiny creature struggled for life. Kate picked up the squirming, slippery fish, and walked into the ocean; placed it in deeper water. 'There you are,' she said.

As the waves threatened her, she ran backward into Michael's arms. He turned her to face him and ran his fingers down her cold cheek. Removing his jacket, he wrapped her in it and pulled her close. She had no objections.

Kate stretched her arms up around his neck. She should be saying goodbye, but his body was hard and warm, and she was trembling, not only from the cold. His cheeky smile told her he knew. She held him tight before pulling away.

Looking around the beach, she thought they were alone, but said, 'We should get back.'

The day out came to an end. Families and friends gathered their belongings, said their goodbyes, and went their separate ways.

The afternoon shadows drew long. The air was still, the wind of the day spent. Kate and Peg trudged up the hilly street while tired, sunburnt children complained to their mothers. Tilly hurried ahead to prepare for her evening out.

Michael Brannigan walked with them. When he lifted the young girl onto his shoulders, she did not protest, and challenged the young boy to a race. Harry, as most boys would, forgot his tiredness and raced ahead up the street.

'He's good with kids. Is he married?' Peg asked.

Kate did not answer.

'Kate?'

Kate looked up the road at the man carrying her child on his shoulders. 'His wife died.'

'Be careful, Kate.'

'You know me.' Kate shrugged her shoulders.

'This is not you,' Peg said.

At the front gate, Harry grinned – he'd won the race – while Michael caught his breath as he swung Jessie down to the ground. The little girl smiled shyly before she opened the gate and skipped to talk to her dog on the front step.

'Come on, Mum,' Harry said as he tugged Peg's arm. 'I'm hungry.'

Chapter Five

Pandemonium reigned as Kate tried to get the younger girl bathed and fed, and the older girl ready for her outing.

Michael sat on the bench on the front veranda, watching the late afternoon sun cast shadows across the road as he listened to the family moving about inside the little house. The sounds brought up memories from the dark place in his mind he had hidden them.

'G'day,' the young man said as he opened the gate and swaggered down the pathway. He wore a grey waistcoat over a blue shirt that was tucked into grey baggy trousers, and his blond hair was slicked down. Michael replied to his greeting as he knocked on the front door.

Tommy emitted a low whistle when he saw Tilly standing before him. Kate scowled at him but could hardly contain her smile. Tilly indeed looked lovely, dressed in a pale green cotton frock, her damp hair accentuating the red curls sitting on her collar. Kate had let her powder her cheeks and use some lipstick for this special occasion.

'Remember, Tommy,' Kate said, 'Tilly must be home by ten-thirty at the latest … and remember, Father Kelly will be there.'

Her last remark caused Tilly to exclaim, 'Oh, Kate!'

'Go on,' Kate said. 'Have a good time.'

She watched as they left her garden, the young man walking a proper distance from his companion. Laughing gently, she sat beside Michael, the dog resting at his feet nudging her leg.

'He's hungry. Come inside; I'll fix his food.'

Michael looked around the sitting room. The furnishings were light and floral, a dark blue rug sat on the polished floor. There were photographs around the room. He recognised some as the people he had met. A small photograph of a man in uniform sat on the Jarrah mantlepiece. Another of this man and Kate on their wedding day.

From the pocket inside his white jacket he took out his leather wallet and removed a small picture. He hadn't had the picture in his hands for a long time. He was looking at it when Kate came into the room with a tray in her hands. He folded the photograph and put it back in the wallet and then into his pocket.

'I'm afraid I only have tea,' Kate said.

'Tea's fine.'

He took the tray from her and put it on the table. They sat together on the floral settee under the front window.

'I'm a bit slow in the queues and missed the coffee last time Stanford's had some,' Kate said and poured the tea.

'She's a pretty young woman,' he said.

'Tilly? Yes, she is.'

'Was it hard for her when her mother died?' He'd never spoken about this.

'She was very young, not quite three, so she doesn't remember much now,' Kate said.

'Karen was six.' Six is old enough to remember, he knew that.

'I wasn't there,' he said. 'I haven't seen her since then.'

He clenched his fists together, and Kate wrapped her hands around them.

He let out a breath.

'It was my fault. I should have let her go; they would still be alive if I hadn't been so selfish.'

'Michael …' Kate held his hands; looked into his eyes. He didn't want to do this. He'd locked the pain away, and he didn't know if he could let it out.

He had to tell Kate.

'I loved her. I thought we were happy. Carol said she wanted to go to the mainland, take the children, spend some time with her sister, think about our life. Why didn't I know this?'

He took his wallet out. His fingers fumbled with the picture. He gave it to Kate. His family, his wife, his little girl with blonde hair and his little boy with dark curly hair.

'I asked her to stay. Wait for me to get back from patrol. We could go together with the children; it could be a Christmas holiday.'

Kate held the picture of his family. He could see the tears she was trying to hide.

'We'd known each other a long time – our fathers were stationed together when we were children. We kept in touch, fell in love, got married, had the children, all the things you do.'

So much to remember. He'd hidden from it for so long it was hard to say the words aloud.

'I thought she knew what to expect. Maybe I should have offered to leave the 'boat'. We were on patrol. We should have been back early in December … we weren't at war then. After the attack on Pearl Harbour everything changed. We didn't get back until January.'

His chest hurt, and he took in slow deep breaths.

'I'd been told. When I got home, everything was gone. The house was empty; my mother had taken my daughter to the mainland. My wife and son were gone.'

His vision blurred.

'The Commodore, Carol's father, told me Carol had been driving on that Sunday. She misjudged a bend in the road and went over the edge; she died instantly. Jamie died in the hospital the next day. My little boy died on his own.'

His head in his hands, he could not stop the tears that fell.

Kate wrapped her arms around him and pulled him close, her tears mingled with his. She let him think.

Then she pushed him away gently and wiped her cheeks with the back of her hand. He should turn away. Men aren't allowed to cry; they have to be strong and brave, not shed tears.

'It was my fault,' he said. 'I should have let her go.'

He had kept his grief locked in that dark place for so long; it exhausted him.

Kate took his face in her hands and wiped his tears away.

'It wasn't your fault, Michael. How could it be?' she asked.

He couldn't speak.

'It was an accident, nobody's fault. Carol must have wanted to stay; otherwise, she would have taken the children and gone to visit her sister. It was a terrible accident.' How many people had said those words to him: Carol's parents, his mother, the Chaplin, Joe Daniels. How many? He had pushed the words away with the memories. Locked them up, buried himself, done what he was expected to do – he looked after his men and served his nation. He had pushed it all away. He didn't want to hear those words then. Why did he listen now? 'I want to remember them, Carol and my little boy.'

'You must, Michael,' Kate said. 'You have to remember them, for you and for your daughter. Karen needs to be able to talk about her mother and brother.'

She pulled him close and said, 'And so do you.'

He remembered. In her arms, he remembered a strength he had forgotten.

A soft tap on the front door disturbed them.

'That will be for me,' he said.

It was nearly dark, the last light from the sun struck the windows opposite and reflected off the black car waiting at Kate's front gate.

On the front veranda, he held his hat in his hands; he wasn't sure, did he have the right to ask her. In her eyes, he saw his answer.

'Can I see you next time we are in port?'

'Please.'

He bent and kissed her softly on the cheek. He wanted more. He wanted to hold her against his body, taste her lips with his, but he needed her consent. He turned to leave.

'Michael,' she whispered.

He took her in his arms and kissed her mouth. Her lips were cracked and dry and tasted of the ocean, but they softened and parted as she responded to his kiss.

***

Kate pulled him close. He was strong and male, the cologne he wore contained nutmeg, cinnamon and citrus. She breathed it in. He ran his tongue around her lips, gently pushing into her mouth. She opened her lips; his tongue was enticing, she wanted more so she kissed him completely.

It was too soon to be in love. Their minds knew that, they were both grown adults, not love-struck youngsters. But their souls knew a longing neither of them thought to feel again. They clung together, feeling the strength of that need.

He peeled himself away, picked up his hat, and walked down the pathway, out the gate, and into the waiting car. Kate stood on the veranda and watched the car drive away.

Chapter Six

Kate had three visitors the next day. One expected, one half expected, and one totally unexpected.

Frank Kelly called in the morning. They shared tea sitting on the wicker chairs on the back veranda. The sun was warm in a blue sky. The morning wind was still, and sounds from the port could be heard.

'How long will you be gone?' Kate asked as she poured the tea.

'I don't know, a while, I think. Probably until it's all over.'

She knew he was tired. He tried to hide it, but they knew each other too well for that. She reached across the table and took his hand. He was pale, his face drawn, his dark hair beginning to go grey at the temples, and his blue eyes no longer sparkled.

Kate said, 'We tried Frank, we did try; peace didn't last long. The boys raced off to war as soon as they could. Did they never think they might not come back?'

Frank shook his head and said, 'Kate, about Michael?'

'He's widowed.'

'Yes, I know. It's about Patrick.'

'I loved Patrick.'

'I know, and he loved you. That's why he asked me to tell you this, as a friend. He said if anything happened to him and you found someone else, he wanted you to be happy. Not mourn for him for the rest of your life, like our mother has done for our father.'

Kate looked into his eyes. The Kelly boys had always been in her life. She was a baby when she moved into the house next door to them. Their fathers, like most of the eligible men, had gone off to war together in 1915, their young families left to look after each other.

Kate's father would not bear arms. He refused to take another life, so he spent his time caring for the wounded. She was lucky he had come home to her. Frank's father had not come home to him – he had become the man of the house at ten years old.

Kate always thought she would marry Frank Kelly until the day he told her he was going to become a priest. Her fifteen-year-old heart shattered into a million pieces. Surprisingly she hadn't died of this broken heart even though she thought she would. And of course, she had grown up and understood his love for God and her love for Patrick.

'Frank, I'm not sure. I loved Patrick. When he died, I thought I would too, but you don't, you just keep going – you have too. I had Jessie. I don't know if I can do that again.'

'My sweet girl,' he said, 'sometimes we have no choice.'

'But I've got to keep us safe. What about Jessie and Tilly. Can we love someone who might leave us on our own again?'

He kissed her hands and said, 'It will be all right.'

She nodded her head. Michael Brannigan had come into her life.

'When do you leave?' she asked.

'Early tomorrow.'

On the front veranda, Frank and Kate held each other tight as they said their goodbyes.

'Take care,' she whispered. 'Come home soon.'

'I will. Be happy, my darling,' he said. He kissed her gently on the cheek.

Kate watched as he walked down the hilly street.

Kate's second visitor was a complete surprise. She was in her front garden pulling weeds out. After the men had gone to war, with food rationed, she had dug out her flower beds and lawn to make space for vegetables. Tomorrow's roses would have to wait until the war was over. Kate did not dig out Patrick's favourite rose bush while he was away, and when he died, she was grateful of that. She was digging around this when she heard the crunch of tyres on the road. She lifted her head as it stopped at her front gate and a burly red hair man in a navy and white uniform stepped out.

'Mrs Kelly,' he said.

'Jack Morgan …' Kate recognised him.

She stood, wiped her hands on her shorts, and opened the gate.

'Lieutenant Brannigan asked me to deliver these to you,' he said, tipping his head at the parcel he carried.

'Nylons and chocolates weren't hard, but the coffee, I had to use all my contacts to find that. Still, I've got to look after my Officer's lady.'

'Officer's lady?'

'That's what he said ma'am. A lady I know has no coffee. Could I find some for her and nylons, so she can share them with Tilly. And chocolates for the little girl.'

Nylons to share with Tilly. Michael must have heard them arguing. Tilly had sulked: why did she have to wear socks? Why couldn't she wear nylons, she was nearly fifteen now. Kate said if she had any she could wear them, but she did not, so she could not.

He put the parcel on the front step, and Kate walked back to the car with him.

'Thank you, Jack.'

''Chief' ma'am,' he corrected her.

'Thank you 'Chief',' Kate said.

Kate watched the car drive away. She was not the only one on the street to do so.

Her hands were dirty, and her knees covered in mud. *An Officer's lady,* she smiled to herself and, returning to the step, sat and opened the envelope on top of the parcel.

> *My Dear Kate,* Michael had written,
>
> *Last night for the first time I knew I could bring memories of my wife and son back into my life. I must share these with Karen.*
>
> *You have reminded me I have the courage I need to do this.*
>
> *I will see you when I return.*
>
> *Michael.*

PS I hope this helps with shop queues.

She wiped the tears from her face with dirty hands and took the parcel inside.

Kate's third visitor called in the evening. The knock on the door was no surprise, and neither was the caller.

'Come in, Jean.' Kate took the younger woman's hand and led her into the kitchen.

'A cup of tea's what we need,' Kate said and went about preparing it.

'Nick's leaving,' Jean said. 'He was supposed to have two weeks leave. We made plans and now he's leaving. It's not fair, Kate.'

'Yes, I know, and no, it's not fair,' Kate said.

Nothing about this war has been fair. She tried to comfort the younger woman. She seemed to be playing this role more often these days, young enough to be a friend, not old enough to a parent.

'You know they're leaving?' Jean said.

No-one should know these things. They were to be kept quiet, and not talked about. Spies were said to be everywhere.

'I know,' Kate repeated. 'Come on, drink your tea. He'll be back soon, you'll see.'

'What if something happens to him? What if he doesn't come back?'

'Why shouldn't he, nothing's happened to him yet. Captain Daniels is very experienced.' Kate's heart pounded so fast; she could hardly hear the words she was saying. Who was she trying to convince?

Drinking tea with a friend is a comfort, but soon it was time for Jean to leave. Kate walked her home, glad of the chance for fresh air and exercise.

Kate did not sleep well. She woke early, pulled on her robe, and sat on her back step overlooking the town. The old dog came and rested his head on her knee. The eastern horizon glowed, the light spreading to the western horizon before the sun's rays broke through the grey sky. Iron rooftops glistened in a fine mist; golden vapor covered the harbour and the ocean. Smoke rose from some chimney tops letting her know she was not alone. The sounds of the day became louder. The horse and cart delivering milk. Trams rumbling along their tracks. An occasion car driving along the high street. The mist over the port caused sounds to echo and amplify. She clearly heard the whistle of a submarine. The Codfish … soon she would go through the heads. Out of the safe harbour. Into the depths of the ocean. Not to see sunshine for days, only surfacing at night to recharge her batteries.

How can they bear it? she thought.

She closed her eyes, seeing faces. *Frank, my dear friend, be careful, be careful, come home soon.* And Michael, she had told Frank she wasn't ready for Michael, but she knew it was almost too late to say that.

She had always been sensible, always had control of her life. Made her own decisions, even before she was on her own. She had kept the promises she made to herself, but she was breaking one of those promises now.

Maybe Frank was right. Sometimes there is no choice.

On Tuesday 19th December 1944, Kate Kelly began a new life.

Chapter Seven

Christmas was celebrated. Family and friends gathered, attended church, prayed, shared a meal, and sang songs. Men continued to die on islands to the north, at places unknow and unheard of, places with strange and exotic names.

Kate and Peg volunteered for the Red Cross. Waited for mail. Queued for rationed food. Swam in the ocean and sat in the sun to tan their skin. The children grew and enjoyed the company of their mothers while missing the company of their fathers.

It was hot. Gardens withered, and the grass turned brown. Patrick's roses burnt and began to die. The searing heat, the old wooden piers and oily waters of the little port had the potential for disaster. On January 17th, 1945, it happened. A careless action of cigarette ash dropped onto an oily rag below the pier, fanned by the updraft, blown into the hold of the SS Panamanian, went unnoticed until the ship was on fire. Sirens wailed, and bells rang. Ships and submarines loaded with weapons moved out to sea.

Kate and her mother stood hand in hand on the back veranda and watched smoke billow over the harbour. They waited for Sean O'Brien to return from the dock where he worked. Twelve hours later, he returned to his wife and daughter, covered in soot, his hair singed but unharmed.

Kate began to notice the sounds of the harbour, searching faces when she was at the dock with the Red Cross. She tried not to think too much, and kept herself busy – you had to keep busy, it was the only way.

Summer holidays ended for the children. Kate and Tilly argued once again about her leaving school. Kate was determined to keep Tilly at school for at least one more year.

The heat of summer intensified. Night after night, the wind blew from the east. There was no sea breeze in the day to cool the land. Then the wind stopped blowing; the days and nights were still and hot.

On Friday morning, the ninth day of February, thick black clouds rolled in across the ocean. Sheets of lightning broke the horizon. Kate was digging up potatoes from the back garden. The hot heavy air stripped her energy. Sweat soaked her clothing. Her head spun but she had to move the potatoes onto the veranda before the rain came. The rumbling thunder was getting closer and forked lightning split the sky. Kate hurried to gather the potatoes and put them in the sack. Rain began to fall, big heavy drops that hit the ground with a plop and caused steam to rise in the dust. With all her strength, she pulled the full sack towards the house. Lightning cut the sky and thunder crashed, shaking the air around her. She closed her eyes and continue tugging the sack. Steady rain wet the dry earth, turning it into mud. Kate slipped and fell. The dog pushed his nose into her knees urging her up.

'Damn, damn, damn.'

The storm surrounded her. Lightning and thunder rocked the earth. She buried her head in her knees and cried, 'Go away. Go away.'

The hands on her arms felt firm and strong as they lifted her from the ground and turned her around. Gentle fingers pushed the hair that had fallen from her green checked scarf out of her eyes. The sky lit up with a roar, and Kate shuddered. Rain was falling; they were getting wet. The dog ran for the safety of his blanket on the veranda.

'Let me help you,' Michael said.

He led her into the house and sat her at the kitchen table. Rain beat on the tin roof and the closed windows. She should get up and open the windows, let the sweet wet air in to cool the house. Michael returned to the kitchen. Kate stared at him – he was there, standing in front of her.

'You're wet,' she said.

'It will dry. You should see yourself.'

A grin spread across his face and wrinkled his eyes. She knew why she had spent all those sleepless nights and these last anxious days.

Kate rose from the chair; she was dirty and smelly; she had waited for his return and now look at her. Stumbling over her words, she raced through the house opening windows to let the fresh air in. The water heater in the bathroom had not been stoked. Kate showered in cold water, grabbed her robe from the back of the bathroom door and wrapped it around her damp body. She returned to the kitchen, drying her hair.

***

Michael had removed his jacket and tie and was sitting at the kitchen table when Kate came into the room. She had been on his mind often. The time he'd spent with her helped him find some peace. He had bought his hidden memories back into his life, his wife and little boy. He was coming to realise he could be the man he used to be. There was hope in his life, and he was anxious to share this with Kate.

She stood before him, a towel in one hand, clutching her robe together with the other. He rose from the chair. 'My beautiful girl,' he said. Kate lowered her eyes; her cheeks turned pink at his words. He traced his fingers around her cheekbones, tilting her chin so she was looking into his eyes. Her blue eyes were almost violet in the kitchen light, the freckles on her nose showed under suntan. She was changing his life. His body reacted to her closeness, and he asked without doubt. 'Make love with me?'

'Now?' He heard the tremble in her voice. 'It's the middle of the day.'

'Now,' he said.

***

Kate lay the towel over the back of the chair and took his hand. As they were leaving the kitchen, she said, 'Wait.'

The gold band on her finger … she had continued to wear it after Patrick's death, now she could not. She removed the ring and placed it on the kitchen table. Michael placed the gold band from his left hand beside it. He wrapped his arm around her waist and held her close as they left the kitchen.

It was stifling in the bedroom. The rain was heavy on the roof; spray flew through the open window carrying the sweet scent of wet grass into the room.

Kate sat at the dresser. She combed and plaited her hair and watched Michael in the mirror as he undressed. He held out his hand, and she went to him. Untying the sash on her robe, he pushed it off her shoulders, took her face in his hands and kissed her lips. His hands moved down her body; he kissed her neck and shoulder. She lifted his face to look in his eyes, kissed him on the forehead, then the mouth. They were overcome and made love urgently.

Kate woke to a familiar sound in an unfamiliar circumstance. She grabbed her robe, shut the bedroom door, and rushed into the kitchen.

'Peg, thank goodness,' she said.

'What's wrong Kate? Are you sick?' Peg asked.

She was in her robe, and her cheeks were hot – no wonder Peg thought she was sick.

'No, no, I'm fine.'

The white jacket on the back of the kitchen chair wasn't easy to miss.

'I'll come back later,' Peg said.

'I'm sorry, Peg. Do you want something?'

'Eggs.'

'I haven't looked yet. Help yourself.'

Two friends stood facing each other.

'Lock the door, Kate,' Peg said.

The clock over the kitchen mantle read eleven-thirty: the girls would not be home until half-past three. The storm had passed.

Kate returned to the bedroom. Michael was dozing. She stood in the doorway. His shoes were neatly tucked under the bed, and his trousers and shirt lay over the back of the chair she kept in the room. What a mess the room would have been if she had ever dared to do anything like this with Patrick Kelly.

He was the only man she had ever been with. They had fumbled around each other's bodies on their wedding night. They had been raised to believe sex was for the making of children, not physical pleasure and enjoyment. It was drummed into them every day of their High School life. Patrick said he didn't believe that, but don't tell Frank, and they had laughed and discovered each other. She was soon pregnant with Jessie, so any guilt she felt had disappeared. She felt no guilt now.

***

Michael opened his eyes. Kate was standing in the doorway. She had come to him so willingly now she seemed unsure. Kate sat on the bed beside him. He put his hands inside her robe; she didn't move; he withdrew his hands.

'Forgive me, Michael, I'm afraid,' she said.

'Did I hurt you?' He couldn't bear to think he might have hurt her but their lovemaking was rushed. He remembered his father telling him, *you're a big boy, Mickey; hold your weight, always be gentle, always be kind.*

'Oh no, Michael, not you, me. Maybe if we were just friends, if …' she said.

'Is that possible?' He took her hands. 'To be just friends?'

She shook her head. 'No.'

Her unspoken fear cut into him. Should he have stayed away?

'I want you in my life, Michael,' she said.

'Nothing's going to happen to me, Kate … understand you have given me every reason to make sure of that. We'll be okay, we know what we are doing … Joe's a good captain.'

Kate untied her robe and pushed it behind her. He wrapped her in his arms and supported as they lay back on the bed. Her body was soft and fragile. He ran his hands over her breasts, across the stretch marks on her stomach and between her legs. She responded to his touch and wrapped her arms around the back of his neck. Running her fingers down his throat, she nibbled his mouth.

He closed his arms around her as they drifted towards sleep. He could feel her heart beating.

***

Kate woke and slowly turned onto her back. Lovemaking in the heat is sticky and sweaty. Michael stood before her, a towel around his waist and rubbing his hair with another.

She stretched her arms above her head. How beautiful he was, his skin so pale, almost white. His brown eyes showed his age. His body was solid and masculine. He amazed her.

'I must get up.' But she didn't move.

'Must you?'

He pulled the sheet from her and dropped the towels on the floor. Climbing onto the bed, he knelt over her clasping her hands above her head.

'Must you?' he repeated.

'Really,' Kate said. 'I must get up.'

She made no effort to move.

'Must get up,' she protested weakly. He kissed her face and neck. Still holding her wrists, he fondled her nipples with his mouth. He released her wrists and moved his mouth down her body, kissing her stomach, her thighs. He was between her legs, and she thought she should stop him, but didn't really want too, her body ached for his. Kate gave him her body.

His breathing became uneven, and he groaned gently. When he came to her, she wrapped her legs around his back, pulling his body into hers. She couldn't hold him any closer or tighter … they would have to share one skin to do that.

***

Michael rolled onto his back; he gently disentangled Kate's limbs from his.

'My goodness,' she said.

She clung to him so desperately during their lovemaking, he really was afraid he might hurt her.

'You are wonderful,' he said.

He always felt restrained when making love with his wife. He felt inhibited by who she was, and perhaps she felt the same – she was after all his boss's daughter. Sometimes he felt she saw him as just another sailor, maybe to be trusted, but maybe not. She had never given him what Kate was giving him, and he had never expected her to. He had known the first time he set eyes on Kate lovemaking would be different, and now he knew how different.

Michael sat at the kitchen table. He wore his trousers and a sweatshirt and watched Kate prepare food. Her plaited hair sat on top of her head. She wore a white skirt and a green checked blouse.

'Are you hungry?' she asked.

She cut bread and spread butter, thinly, before spreading a thick black greasy substance on the slices. Kate poured coffee and sat opposite him.

'I'm starving,' she said.

She took a slice of bread and drank her coffee. He screwed his face up. And she giggled. 'It's Vegemite … it's good, try some.'

It looked like axle grease, but she seemed to like it, so he took a piece and tasted it.

'Thank you for the coffee and nylons. You shouldn't have troubled yourself.'

'I wanted too,' he replied.

He had no doubts about his feelings for her. He knew she saw his life as dangerous. Sometimes it was. Sometimes it was terrifying, but he saw it as no different to anyone else fighting this war. It was the life he had chosen. He liked getting his hands dirty, not commanding from a distance. He found the technology and science involved in submarines intriguing.

His Captain and friend Joseph Daniels, a brilliant man, had finished top of their class at the Academy in '35. When the Codfish was commissioned in'38, Joe took command of her. He had been honoured to come aboard as second in command.

He did understand her fears and wished he could make them disappear – she had given him so much in such a short time. He was coming to accept the death of his wife and son was an accident, and he was not to blame. He could now think of the time they had spent together, and the few precious years he had with his little boy. This was because of Kate. One day they would talk about it, but for now he ate the strange food she offered him as she asked about Frank Kelly.

'He got away safely. We dropped him at the rendezvous; men from his unit met him. He is important to you?'

'Yes, he is my friend. I've known him ever since I was a little girl. He loved me, but he loved God more, and I married Patrick.'

***

Kate took his hand. Could she put into words how he made her feel? 'I have you now,' was all she could say. She knew he would understand.

'And I have you,' he said.

There was so much to tell each other, but it was getting late. Kate said, 'The girls will be home soon.'

He said he should go; she asked him to stay.

'Not yet. Can I take you all out tonight?' he asked.

'Peg and I usually take the children to the beach for tea on Friday. Nothing fancy, just fish from the fishmonger. Will that be all right?'

'I'll call at 18.00 hours, is that okay?'

She stared at him blankly.

'Sorry. Six o'clock.'

Chapter Eight

Jessica Kelly sat beside her mother and looked at the man sitting opposite her. Mummy said you remember Lieutenant Brannigan and he said my name is Michael. She thought maybe she should remember him. Mummy seemed happy that he was with them. She sat under young Norfolk Pine trees; the grass scratched her legs. And she remembered she had liked him when carried her up the hill, on that hot day after the beach. But he never came back to see them, and she forgot about him.

What a strange day. The awful storm made her cry, and the boys teased her, but Sister Mark let her sit by her desk. When she came home, Mummy seemed different, then this strange man visited. Now he was looking at her; he had a nice smile, she might like him.

'Finished?' Kate asked.

'Yes,' Jessie answered.

The cool evening air was heavy with salt. The sun's rays pushed their way through the last of the storm clouds with gold and silver arrows. People walked or sat on the grassed esplanade. The High Street was crowded with families and friends enjoying the cool break from the summer's heat. The rain had washed the buildings clean; the lawns and gardens sparkled; the dust of the hot summer washed away.

Families stood on the wet terrace of the War Memorial and looked out over the town to the ocean and the setting sun; the monument, a tribute to those who had lost their lives in previous wars, could be seen from all parts of the township and out to sea. The surrounding gardens were immaculate and watered even in most severe heat waves.

Jessie and Harry chased each other around on the green grass. Tilly, too old for their game of 'chasey', watched them play. Soon the children returned their mothers and Peg started for home with them.

***

Kate stood with her back to Michael. The sun set, a huge gold ball disappearing into the ocean. All the colours of the rainbow swirled together through the clouds. The sky was turning pink, even to the eastern horizon.

She pulled his arms around her. The light of the day was fading; it would be dark soon; there was no twilight here.

'No regrets?' he asked.

'No regrets.'

She turned to face him, took his face in her hands, and bought his lips to hers.

'Disgraceful.' She heard a female voice. 'In a public place with a bloody 'Yank'. Whore.'

Kate pulled away and turned to see a group of women walking nearby. She knew she had broken the boundaries of what was socially acceptable by kissing Michael in public. She also knew it was of little importance to her anymore. What was important was the man who held her in his strong, protective arms. He turned her around to face him so she couldn't see the approaching women. She didn't need him to do that; she could look after herself. But she knew he needed to do that for her, so she stayed in his embrace. To have such a word said about them! She would let herself lean on Michael for a little bit.

Kate understood how some people thought. You were considered to be letting 'our Australian boys' down if you went out with an American serviceman. You were supposed to save yourself for when they came home.

It hadn't been like that when the American fleet arrived in Fremantle. They were welcomed and viewed almost as saviours. There had always been some animosity between the men of the different nations, mostly bar room fighting that was quickly bought under control by the Military Police.

It was different now. The American servicemen had a lot more money than most Australian servicemen. They were able to obtain many items the Australians could not. As the war dragged on and Australian men returned injured or did not return, feelings of resentment appeared and deepened.

Her husband was one of those who would not return. And this man who held her in the shelter of his arms put his life in danger fighting the common enemy.

She said, 'Not everyone's the same, Michael.' Her words muffled in his chest.

'They are not,' he agreed. He shielded her with his body as the group of women passed.

'Okay?' he asked when they were alone.

'Yes,' she replied. 'Let's go home now.'

On the pathway heading down Solomon Street, Peg and the children were a shadowy group. The old dog wandered slowly on his own. Kate stroked him under the chin, 'Poor boy wouldn't they wait for you?' He looked at her with his old eyes. Kate would always wait for her beloved pet.

'Come on then.'

The dog walked slowly beside Kate. Michael walked on the other side of him.

'He's very old?' Michael asked.

'Yes, I've had him since I was fifteen – he is very old now. Pat and I found him in the river where someone had thrown him in to die. Pat swam out to get him. His mum wouldn't let him keep him. We hid him for two weeks before my dad found him. I talked dad into letting me keep him. His name is Sam.'

Michael took her hand, and the dog moved to one side, allowing him to walk beside Kate.

'Just memories,' she said.

She put her arm around Michael's waist, and they held each other as they walked home.

'Mummy?' Jessie asked as Kate put her to bed. 'Is 'Tenant Michael going to live with us?'

Kate answered honestly, 'He will be visiting us. He is a special friend of Mummy's. I hope you will like him.'

'Yes, mummy,' the child replied. 'I love you, mummy.'

'And I love you. Time for bed now. Goodnight.'

She tucked the sheets around her daughter and thought it might be difficult for Jessie to relate to Michael. The only man she saw regularly was her grandfather, and she loved him very much.

In the front room, Michael had removed his jacket and tie. He lay on the settee, his eyes closed, asleep. Kate did not disturb him; she was quite weary herself. She covered him with a light blanket from her bed and stood watching him sleep. Her eyes would not stay open. It was time for her to go to bed.

Kate and the girls slept late. After so many hot, sleepless nights, it was a pleasure that would not last long. When she rose, Kate made the best of the cool morning. She chopped wood, stoked the water heater, and prepared breakfast before the girls joined her.

'Is 'Tenant Michael gone?' Jessie asked. She rubbed her eyes as she sat at the kitchen table.

'Yes,' Kate answered.

'Is he coming back?'

'Yes.'

'Do you like him?' Tilly asked. She poured herself a cup of tea and then sat at the table.

'Yes,' Kate answered.

'A lot?' A question only a not quite grown woman could ask.

'Yes, Tilly,' Kate said. 'A lot.'

Michael returned just before midday. Kate was collecting eggs. She heard Jessie and Michael talking as they walked around the side of the house. The cool respite was nearly over. The noonday sun shone in a clear sky. The garden had enjoyed the rain, the dust of summer washed away, the plants stood tall and colourful.

'Look, mummy, look what 'Tenant Michael bought for me and Tilly,' Jessie said. She ran to show her mother the small posies she held.

'Can I put them in water?' Jessie asked.

'Can you manage?'

'Yes.' Clutching her flowers, Jessie ran up the back steps into the house.

Kate and Michael stood facing each other. She held a bowl of eggs in her hands. Her straw hat sat on the back of her head, and she wore her white shorts and her green checked blouse. Michael was out of his white uniform: he now wore khaki. From behind his back, he took a single white rose.

'For you,' he said.

The eggs in her basket shook as she took the rose in one hand. He took the bowl from her and placed it on the ground. Then he took her hands kissing her fingertips before he pulled her close.

Small feet crunched dirt as they ran around the side of the house, and they pulled apart.

'Jessie, Jessie,' Harry Kennedy called. He ran around the house, up the stairs, slamming the back door behind him.

'Boys,' Peg said as she followed her son. 'Always in a hurry.'

'Yes,' Kate said. She held Michael's arm tight as he watched the little boy with dark curly hair race into the house.

***

Matilda O'Brien returned to a house full of noise and chatter. Jessie ran to show her the flowers. She blushed and thanked Michael shyly. *He seems like a nice man,* she thought. *I will probably get to like him.*

She was surprised when her friend May's mother asked questions about Michael. She hadn't thought anyone else knew he was visiting. Tilly told her that he was the same man who called before Christmas. He had come home with them last night and was

gone in the morning. She wondered why May's mum needed to
know that.

51

Chapter Nine

The Pier Hotel on Collie Street, Fremantle was operated by Amanda Collins, a robust woman in her late forties. It was a small establishment, not far from the docks. The sturdy building was made from iron and stone. Downstairs there was a public bar for men only. There was also a lounge and dining room where ladies and gentlemen were served. On the next floor up, there were ten rooms and the necessary ablution amenities.

All these rooms were occupied at the moment. Since the arrival of the Submarine Fleet, the rooms were often full, billeted out to the officers. Captain Joseph Daniels and his officers had been using the Pier Hotel on and off for the past three years. Captain Daniels was well-liked by the staff of the Pier Hotel. He was handsome, confident, polite and friendly, and he kept strict control of his Junior Officers. The hotel was always quiet when he was there.

***

Kate and Michael sat at a table in the dining room; Joseph Daniels sat reading by a window. They were the only occupants of the hotel at the moment.

Kate, her hair clipped loosely behind her ears, wore her blue frock and navy-blue jacket. Michael wore his white uniform. They ate their meal – much of which Kate hadn't been able to afford or obtain for many years – talking quietly. Holding hands over the table, they played with each other's fingers. After their meal, they left the table and went upstairs, ignoring the sign at the bottom of the staircase about guests in rooms.

Upstairs the open window let in the salt-laden air. The browned-out table lamp cast shadows on the walls. Green checked cotton curtains moved in the breeze. Kate and Michael clung together, longing for the closeness of lovemaking, unwilling to accept it was over until they finally lay quietly in each other's arms.

Kate lifted her head from Michael's chest, and he asked, 'You are happy?'

She never thought she could be truly happy after Patrick's death. She thought the empty space his death caused would never leave her. But Michael was filling that space. She had broken the promises she had made to herself, broken all the rules she had put in place for herself. Let him into her life and into her heart. It frightened her how quickly that had happened.

'Yes, Michael, I am happy,' she said.

She would grasp the time they had, and share it; she could be happy. Life went on around the war and one day there would be peace again. One day there would be happiness without fear.

'You are?' she asked.

***

Michael never expected to fall in love again; he thought that part of him died with his wife and child. His love for his daughter kept him sane, and one warm December day, he met this beautiful woman who lay in his arms.

He could be happy again. 'Yes,' he said. 'I am.'

Kate said, 'Tell me about you.'

'What would you like to know?'

'What were you like as a little boy? Did people move their valuable ornaments out of your reach when you came visiting? Your family, do you have any brothers and sisters, your parents?'

Michael pushed the hair that had fallen across her face away. He knew more about her than she did him, and he knew there was still much to learn, but what could possibly matter. Still, she had asked, so he said, 'Did people move valuable ornaments when you came visiting?'

'I've heard such stories,' she said. 'And you?'

'Not that I've heard, but for you, I'll ask Mother. As for the rest, I have no brothers or sisters. My father was the fourth son in his family. He wasn't interested in politics or his family's business, so he joined the Navy. He was away a lot when I was young, but we had fun when he was home. He died when I was seventeen. I tried to help mother with her business, but like my father, the Navy was where I was meant to be. I enjoy the ocean and boats. I have my own little skip at home. Carol and I married and had the children …' He hesitated.

'I'm sorry, Michael,' Kate said.

'No,' he said as he caressed her cheek with his fingers. 'It's okay. I want to talk about Carol and Jamie now. They are part of my life, my past, they will always be there, and because of you, I can think of them. I have my daughter, who I cherish, and now I have you. Do you understand?'

She nodded yes, but he wondered if she understood what she meant to him; if she understood how she had taken him out of the dark place he was in, how he was coming back to life. He took her face in his hands, bringing her close. She wrapped her body around his, and they made love slowly and gently until they slept peacefully together.

Michael woke to find Kate sitting in the bed beside him, the sheet pulled up under her chin. The morning light brightened the room and the easterly wind blew the curtain about. He ran his fingers down her spine, and she turned to him and said, 'I can't do this.'

'You already have.'

'But the girls?'

'They'll be okay.'

When he'd asked Peg if she could mind the girls so he could take Kate out last night, he never intended to keep her out overnight, but it was done now.

'It was wonderful,' she said.

'Yes,' he agreed.

'But I must get home now.'

'Of course.'

'Come stay with us, Michael, while you're here. Stay with us at home.'

He could see how much she wanted that. 'I can't do that.' He remembered the savage words spoken only yesterday. He tried not to let them bother him; tried to keep them out of his mind. He couldn't comprehend how Kate could be seen like that. 'It would hardly be correct with the girls.'

'And this is?'

'This just happened.'

'Yes, it did,' she agreed.

'I will be with you when I can,' he said.

'But the nights, on your own?'

'I will be kept busy, I have letters to write and my duties to perform, and Joe needs my company.'

'Yes, of course, he does.'

'Breakfast.' A young female voice called, with a knock on the door. He shrugged. Breakfast was usually served in the dining room. He swung his legs over his side of the bed, stretched his back, and Kate ran her fingers down his spine. He turned to her kissing her mouth.

'Breakfast,' she mumbled as she returned his kiss.

'Mmm …'

'Go … go get it,' Kate said and pushed him gently away.

She lay back under the sheet and watched as he pulled on his shorts and sweatshirt before he opened the door.

On the floor outside was a tray containing breakfast for two. Michael noticed the tray also contained the strange spread Kate had given him. This was not served at their meals. He smiled to himself at Amanda Collins' kindness; picked up the tray and returned to the bed. 'Breakfast,' he said.

Kate sat; ran her hands through her tangled hair and the sheet fell to her waist.

'Kate,' he scolded, 'this really won't do.'

She did not blush or cover herself. The love in her eyes stopped him where he stood. She had given him back his life, and he knew he would protect her with it. He kissed her forehead and handed her the tray, then he reached into his kit bag and removed a shirt.

'You'd better put this on, or we'll never eat.'

Kate took the khaki sweatshirt and pulled it over her head. 'Better?'

'A little,' he said and sat beside her.

'Do you do this often?' she asked as she indicated the two cups.

'No, never, never.' He was worried for a second, but she was laughing at him, and then with him. They shared their breakfast, and he ate the strange spread she seemed to like and wonder whashe saw in it.

'I must get home to the girls,' Kate said. 'You will come?'

'Yes,' he replied

'Mum and dad are expecting the girls and me for tea tonight, please come and see them.'

He wasn't sure of that, but she had asked him, so he said. 'Okay.'

***

Kate rose from the bed and the sweatshirt fell to her knees. It was time to go home. She took her hairbrush from her handbag and stood in the open window, untangling her hair. Michael kissed her on the back of the neck, and she turned to him. 'Michael, I …'

'I know,' he said. Then he left her and went across the hallway to the bathroom.

Kate looked out over the rusty iron rooftop. She had loved Patrick Kelly, but she always kept a little of herself for herself. Maybe that was how she survived his death. After Jessie was born, she discovered there was another layer to falling in love.

She was holding nothing back from Michael. She was giving him everything. And he would leave her; he would go back to sea. Her hands were clenched on the windowsill keeping her upright.

Church bells were ringing – it was Sunday. She had missed Mass with her family, that could be difficult to explain. But when she arrived home with Michael words would be unnecessary. Closing her eyes, she felt the warm sun on her face and remembered what the Nuns at school had said about sex and marriage all those years ago. None of it mattered now because of Michael.

It was time for Kate to tidy herself up. She had not planned to stay out all night, so she would have to freshen up what she wore last night. As she pushed the bathroom door open, she thought she heard Michael call her name, but it was too late. She stood dumbstruck in the doorway facing Joseph Daniels. He stood at the bathroom sink, naked except for a towel around his waist. His face covered in lather, he held a razor in his hand. He returned her gaze warmly and said, 'Good morning, Kate.'

'Sorry, Kate,' Michael said.

He turned her around, pulled the bathroom door shut, and ushered her back to his room.

'Sorry.'

He held her arms and bent to look in her face. She was startled to see Joe in the bathroom, but the worried look on Michael's face caused her to laugh and say. 'I'll live.'

'Finished,' Joe called from the hallway.

It was mid-morning when Kate and Michael left the bedroom. She felt reasonably presentable in her blue halter dress; she carried her navy jacket. Her summer tan complimented her face, and her dark hair was plaited down her back. The hotel which was nearly empty last night seemed surprising full this morning, and she knew many eyes were on her.

The Junior Officers of the submarine Codfish were making no secret of their interest in her. Michael was their commanding officer. He would be the one they took their problems and ideas too. He would be the one who stood between them and their Captain. He would also be the one to discipline them if they needed. But at the moment they were all too interested in her and not at all shy about showing it.

'Join me for coffee?' Joe Daniels asked.

Kate and Michael joined him at a table by the window, Kate thinking *we should have gone straight home*. But she did want to see Joe, and smiled to herself when she remembered seeing him earlier. He returned her smile. The giggle she was trying to contain spilled over, and with a twinkle in his eyes he joined her laughter. They laughed and talked and enjoyed each other's company.

Chapter Ten

Kate and Michael walked through the small port town. The midday sun was hot in a blue sky, the usual cooling breeze not blowing. They walked arm in arm despite the looks given to them by some they passed. It was Sunday; she told Michael she must go to church.

St Patrick's Catholic Church on Adelaide Street was only forty years old, but it appeared much older. Designed to look like a fourteenth-century Gothic church, it was made from local limestone. The turret columns and window surrounds were made from stone shipped across the country from Sydney.

Kate entered the building alone. It was cool inside, the fragrance of wood and burning candle scented the air. The pictures of the stations of the cross on the walls and the statue of Mary and child … the laws of this church once so important to her … She placed her hand in the water to her right, made the sign of the cross, genuflected beside the pew before she knelt to pray.

Kate had no hat for her head, not even a scarf, but she wondered if that matter so much now. She was already breaking rules – the church did not approve of sex outside of marriage. Jesus had forgiven Mary Magdalene. Kate looked at the carving of the man hanging on the wooden cross above the altar and knew she did not need or want forgiveness.

***

Michael stood on the porch, his hat in his hand. He did not attend church, but it would be disrespectful to stand with his hat on. He turned as the large wooden doors were opened by an elderly man in a black robe.

'Don't stand in the doorway, son,' the priest said. 'Everyone's welcome, come inside.'

'I'm just waiting for someone,' he said.

'Come in out of the heat. We can wait for her inside.'

The wooden doors opened, and Kate joined him and the priest on the step. She introduced him to Father Morgan O'Reilly.

'Have you had any word from Father Kelly?' Father O'Reilly asked.

'No, Father,' Kate answered.

'We dropped him off at the rendezvous, Sir,' Michael said. 'He was fit and well, and men from his unit were there to meet him. That was four weeks ago.'

'You are from the submarine?'

'Yes, Sir.'

'Thank you, Lieutenant,' the priest said. 'I'll be leaving you now. Goodbye, Kate, and you, Lieutenant.'

Michael and Kate stood on the porch and watched the old priest walk around the side of the building.

She said, 'He has a special love for Frank and Patrick. Their mother kept house for him; the boys grew up under his wing, the sons he could not have. Maybe that's why Frank became a priest; he is a gentler soul than Patrick, but Father O'Reilly loved them both.'

'As you do?'

'Yes.' Her hand on his arm told Michael everything he needed to know.

***

Jessica Kelly ran into her mother's arms. She'd been sitting on Aunty Peg's front veranda waiting for Mummy; she didn't mind sleeping at Aunty Pegs: it was fun; she was allowed to stay up late, and got to play with Harry, but it was getting late. Mummy usually came over for breakfast — she hadn't even taken them to church today. She was home now and hugging her, and 'Tenant Michael was with Mummy. She wriggled out of her mother's arms and ran inside the house to tell everyone.

Kate exchanged glances with Michael. There was no need to explain to Jessie, but the red-haired girl leaning on the veranda post was another matter.

'Good afternoon, Tilly,' Kate said and kissed the girl on the cheek.

'Good afternoon, Kate,' Tilly replied stiffly. She did not return Michael's smile and turned and walked back into the house.

Sunday evening meal at Kate's parent's home was different. Her father struggled to hide his feelings when Michael offered his hand. Kate wasn't a little girl, but she loved her father and needed him to at least understand about Michael. She could see it was going to be hard for him to do that. She knew her mother would be the peacemaker, as always.

Kathleen O'Brien dusted her hands on her apron. She took both of Michael's hands in hers and said, 'Welcome home, Michael. It is good to see you again.'

The table was set with the best her mother could find. Jessie was excited and chatting away, Tilly sullen and noncommittal. Kathleen made conversation, which her husband finally joined in. Kate was unusually quiet, and Michael joined in the conversation when it was direct at him.

Chapter Eleven

Michael called every day after the girls had gone to school. Sometimes he came in a taxi. Other times, if he'd been on duty or was going on duty, he would use the black car. Mostly he walked. He tried to avoid gossip and would stay a respectable distance from Kate as they left her home and walked down the street. He chopped wood for Kate; she sat in the sun and watched him, his pale skin gradually tanning. They went swimming and lay on the warm sand to dry themselves.

He took her shopping, and she helped him buy gifts for his mother and daughter, gifts that would be noticed as different to those he usually sent: sizes that fitted and colours that suited. He wanted to buy gifts for Kate and the girls. She would not let him do that, relenting over some ribbons for Jessie's hair, and she let him buy her one pair of nylons to share with Tilly.

They enjoyed making love in the morning or the afternoon, and they talked and learnt about each other.

He took Kate to lunch with Joe Daniels, and they greeted each other with hugs and kisses. He lunched with the Commodore and invited Kate to attend a social function at one of the elegant houses on the riverfront. She declined but insisted he attend. The flirting of the ladies no longer bothered him, and he enjoyed the company of his fellow officers but was happy to return to Kate the next day.

When the girls came home from school, he went walking with them, and they got to know each other. On Saturday, he took Jessie and Harry fishing. He wrote letters, performed his duties, and kept Joe company.

The sun shone every day. The temperature rose, and the cooling winds struggled to keep the days pleasant. Two weeks went by.

Kate Kelly had spent the fastest two weeks of her life. Suddenly it was Sunday, the day before Michael was due to leave. He would go back on board the Codfish, early Monday morning, and then they would be leaving.

Kate was at peace with her God over her love for Michael. She took the girls to Mass with her family on Sunday morning, and Michael joined her. They stood and sat and knelt as required.

Michael offered his hand to her father. Kate knew her father was still unsure of Michael. He was a sailor after all, but he shook the hand offered and held it firmly. She also knew her mother could see Michael had given his heart to her and would always make him welcome.

Mary Kelly did not try to conceal her unhappiness about Michael. He said it was only natural, and she would come to understand in time. Kate shook her head at that.

Kate had planned a day out. After church, she packed sandwiches and tea in the hamper. They travelled by ferry along the winding river into the city. Alighting at a pier, a walk along the riverbank took them to a steep staircase, which led into Kings Gardens.

The garden overlooked the city of Perth. The park was an array of formal gardens and natural bush. A monument to those who had died in previous wars stood in the manicured gardens. From the monument, the river wound into an open waterway with Catalina flying boats taking off and landing.

Over the rooftops, to the east of the small city, hills could be seen. The eucalyptus trees on the escarpment gave a dark, almost blue, colour to the landscape.

The picnic was eaten under tall gum trees that stretched up into a perfect, clear blue sky. Ice cream was bought from the small café in the park. Kate and Michael walked with Jessie swinging between them. When she grew bored with that, they held each other tight, no longer caring if anyone objected. Tilly had her own companion,

Tommy Ingram, and he boldly took her hand as they walked around the gardens.

Too soon, the day out came to an end. Kate and Michael returned to a ferry crowded with servicemen and civilians. The ferry made its way back down the river to the harbour town. The perfect day remained so; there was no wind blowing the water about. The clear blue sky was now tinged with orange as the evening drew nearer.

Kate stood wrapped in Michael's arms; she held them tight around her and leant into his body. They were not alone; other couples were breaking codes of conduct. No one seemed to mind on this crowded vessel.

'Kate …' Michael turned her to face him. 'Kate, will you marry me?'

'Michael,' she whispered.

She felt unsteady on her feet. Had the ferry hit a wave? Her eyes filled with tears – she had promised no tears today, only happiness on his last day of leave.

'You don't have too,' she said.

He dropped his head in mock anguish. He sat her on an empty seat, knelt on one knee in front of her, clasped his hands together and said, 'I, Michael James Brannigan, a thirty-six-year-old Lieutenant Commander in the United States Navy, ask you, Kate Kelly, to be my wife. I have a daughter. I can offer you a home …'

His face became serious. He reached into his pocket and took out a small felt box.

'I love you, Kate. I see no future for me without you.'

He was kneeling in front of her, the little felt box in his hand open. 'Don't you love me?' he asked.

The woman Kate was sitting next to said, 'Don't turn him down. He loves you … look at him.'

Michael was still kneeling in front of her; she hadn't given him an answer.

'Yes, Michael, I love you,' she said

He placed the ring on her finger. It was a perfect fit.

'I love you,' she repeated.

He stood her up and kissed her.

She could hear her girls in the background wanting to know what was happening; could hear clapping and cheering. Then she heard a male voice say, 'Way to go, Sir.'

***

Michael Brannigan pulled the woman he loved close and kissed her passionately on the deck of a crowded ferry. He heard the clapping and cheering; heard the comment. When he turned around, he saw Emerson and other members of his crew watching him and his lady. *My lady,* he thought.

This was not proper behaviour for an officer in front of his men. He loosened his embrace, but he did not remove it. He stood beside the railing with his arms around Kate for the rest of the journey.

***

Jessica Kelly sat on the settee with 'Tenant Michael. He was reading to her, but she wasn't listening. She was sad because he was leaving, and she asked, 'Will you come back and see us soon?'

'Yes, Jessie.'

'Will you stay with us then?'

'After,' he said.

'After what?' She screwed up her face.

'Michael and Mummy are going to get married,' her mother said from the armchair beside the empty fireplace.

Mummy had shown her the ring 'Tenant Michael had given her on the way home. She didn't really know what it meant.

Jessie looked from her mother to Michael. 'When?' she asked.

'Soon,' Michael replied.

'Will you be my daddy then?' she asked.

She didn't remember having a daddy. She knew her daddy was in a picture on the mantlepiece with mummy. She knew he was never coming back. She didn't remember ever seeing him.

'Will that be okay?' he said.

Jessie thought about this for a short time. 'Yes.' She pulled his face to her and kissed his cheek.

***

Tilly O'Brien sat on the other lounge chair, writing to her father. She wrote to him every week, putting each letter in an envelope ready to post when he wrote and told her where to send them. She looked at Jessie and Michael. Jessie's daddy had died in the war, but she didn't know where her daddy was. She pushed herself out of the chair and fled the room, her books and papers scattering on the floor. She ran out onto the back veranda, Kate following her.

'I want my daddy,' Tilly wept.

***

Michael ran his fingers through Kate's hair as she rested her head on his chest after lovemaking. He had always returned to the hotel at night, but tonight he did not. He had to leave early, long before the girls would be awake. He had been very correct in front of them, except for that one night he kept Kate out. He did not want to have them subjected to questions they could not answer; questions that were only his and Kate's to answer.

'I hope we can get married next time I'm in Port.'

'Yes.' She curled close into his chest.

'There is paperwork to arrange.'

'Paperwork?' Kate mumbled.

'We have to get permission to marry local girls.'

'Really?' Kate sat up and pulled the sheet over her.

'Afraid so.'

'You're a grown man, Michael.'

'Yep, rather stupid really,' he said.

He kept his tone light and said. 'I don't think Joe will object, do you?'

'No, I suppose not.'

He noticed her concern. 'We will be married, Kate, no matter what.'

He knew she was yet to fully understand what she meant to him. That was okay, but he was tired now. He pulled her close and held her tight as they drifted to sleep.

***

Kate sat on the bed, her knees tucked under her chin, her fingers laced together around her shins. She watched Michael dress. The light from the sunrise that was to come pushed its way around the edge of the blackout curtains. There could be no tears now; she must keep that promise not to cry while he was with her. When he left the room to retrieve his jacket, she rose, pulled her robe on, and ran her hands through her tangled hair, pushing it behind her shoulders. She joined him in the doorway of her bedroom and took his hand. They looked in on the sleeping occupants in the other bedroom.

***

Michael had said goodbye to the girls last night. Jessie had cried when he tucked her into bed, and he had trouble keeping a brave face. He missed his children … his little boy who he could now remember but who would never grow old, and his daughter growing up without him. Jessie, a little girl with brown curly hair and freckles on her nose, had filled an empty space within him, and he had grown to love her very quickly. The older girl was shy of him and missed her own father, but he hoped they would be friends.

The last stars of the night were fading as the light on the horizon grew brighter. A black car came up Solomon Street; the driver parked the vehicle and turned the lights off.

On the front veranda, he said, 'I love you, and I will be back. Please don't worry.'

Those words were in vain, and there were words he needed to say. He put his hat on and went down the two steps to the pathway. He turned to face her. She was on the top step, her arm outstretched as she held his hand, he had to leave.

67

'Kate,' he said. 'Please be careful. Be here when I get back.'

***

Kate went down the steps into his arms. She could see him trying to hide his fear, trying to hide that memory.

'Yes, yes, my darling, I will be careful,' she said. 'And I will be here when you return. I promise you that.'

She wrapped herself around him, to be part of him a little bit longer.

He pulled himself away. The dog followed him down the pathway. At the gate, Michael bent and rubbed the dog under the chin, then he opened the gate and stepped into the car.

The old dog returned to Kate. He pushed into her legs, demanding attention, and she shuddered. 'What's the matter, boy?' she asked. Kate sat heavily on the top step, her hands in her mouth. Where were the tears she'd been holding back? He was gone: she could cry now.

The dog started whimpering. Kate gasped for air. What was happening, she couldn't breathe, she was drowning, she couldn't reach the surface. She had never experienced anything like this before. Could she survive? She had no choice.

'What do you know, boy? What do you know?' she asked her much loved pet. Kate put her arms around his old neck and buried her face in his fur.

***

Michael Brannigan gave his crew orders and took orders from his Captain. The crew of the submarine Codfish – *his* crew – looked reasonably fit and healthy. There were a few black eyes and split lips, some bleary eyes, and bloated faces.

It must have been a good leave, no serious trouble, or he would have heard from the 'Chief'. His thoughts were of Kate as he surveyed his crew. How quickly she had become part of his life and how right his life was now she was in it. It was difficult to say goodbye this morning. He knew he had to shake the fear for her safety away; he could not let it shadow their life together. She would take care, and she would be waiting for him when he returned. He had to know that.

It was time for him to get back to his duty. As he passed two sleepy-eyed seamen on his way to the torpedo bays, he wondered if his appearance showed any signs of how he'd spent his leave.

Chapter Twelve

There are times that, no matter how old you are, there is only one person to see and one place to go, and Kate did this.

***

Kate walked down the lane at the back of her home; around the corner into another lane and opened a back gate. In the garden vegetables grew in patches among flower beds; grapevines grew on a trellis against the washhouse. A bomb shelter sat in the soil, the tin roof only just visible. A big gum tree stood tall and strong in the middle of the yard. Up the four steps onto the veranda, the flyscreen no longer creaked as she opened it.

Her mother, dark hair streaked with silver, tied in a bun at the nape of her neck, her deep blue eyes, sharp and bright, stood at the stove.

'Tea's made. I thought you might call,' Kathleen O'Brien said. 'Are you all right?'

'I'm okay, mum.' *Okay* – when had that word entered her vocabulary.

'Michael's leaving?' Kathleen asked.

'Soon. They'll be leaving soon.'

***

Kathleen O'Brien poured tea for her daughter and placed the cup in front of her. She liked Michael Brannigan. He was always polite, and his love for her daughter was obvious. She was still having a hard time convincing her husband. But he loved his daughter, and he was starting to understand how much Kate's happiness depended on Michael. Such a fragile happiness.

'You love him very much, and he loves you, you must hold on

to that,' she said.

Kathleen took her daughter's hand and looked at the diamond sitting on a gold band.

'He wants us to be married,' Kate said.

'Of course, he does.'

'When he comes home.'

'He will be all right, Kate,' Kathleen said firmly. 'Now drink your tea.'

Doing as she was told, Kate said, 'I loved Patrick, Mum. It hurt when he left – I cried. I can't cry now. Why can't I cry?'

'Maybe it's different.'

'Maybe. It shouldn't be so hard.'

'No, it shouldn't. But when you have both lost someone you love, when you fall in love again so unexpectedly and so completely… Maybe it's more than being in love.' Maybe that wasn't a good thing.

She looked into her daughter's eyes – her own eyes. Kate had always been sensible, level-headed, and capable. She saw her stiffen.

'Michael,' Kate whispered.

'He will be safe,' she said.

'Yes, we will,' Kate replied. She shook her head. 'He will.'

The submarine moved away from the dock, tugs pulling her from her moorings, guiding her through the harbour. The anti-submarine gates would open and close. Then she would turn north to follow the coast before submerging.

Kate had seen submarines leave when she was doing her Red Cross duty. Michael and Joe were proud, brave men, living a life they had chosen. That life had been overtaken by circumstances, and now they fought for their country and protected their Allies.

She was part of that life now.

On Monday, the twenty-sixth of February 1945, the United States Submarine Codfish left the safety of Fremantle Harbour in Western Australia.

Chapter Thirteen

Kate's old dog died towards the end of March, and she wept unashamedly. The girls cried, and they buried him in the back yard, marking his grave with a cutting from Patrick's rose bush. Kate woke in a panic early the next morning and put it down to her pet's death. It could be nothing else.

Tilly continued to write to her father, and now she wrote to her young friend as well. He could receive her letters.

Mary Kelly never called, and Jessie wanted to see her grandmother. Kate did not want to explain.

Men continued to die on islands to the north. The names on the wireless were monotonous and fearful.

Prison camps were liberated in Europe. The horrors of war, the cruelty that humans can inflict, became apparent. Fear for the safety of prisons known to be held in Singapore and Malaya began to seep into people's lives.

Jean left for the United States. Kate and her family farewelled Jean at the city station. The train journey would take her and many other young brides, some with children, across the country, where they would board a ship for their new homes. Kate stood on the platform with the crowd pushing into her as she waved and repeated promises to keep in touch, the steam from the engine blowing the words away.

Peg began to look for the postman.

Now, on the 3rd day of April 1945, Kate sat on the kitchen floor holding her sobbing friend.

'Come on,' Kate said. 'Come on now.'

Kate helped Peg to her feet, sat her at the table. She put the kettle on, picked up the broken china, made the tea, and put a cup into her friend's hands.

'Would you like me to stay?' Kate asked.

'No, I want to be alone.'

'I'll keep Harry tonight.'

'Please.'

'Is there anything else you need?'

'No,' Peg answered slowly. 'Maybe the telegram's wrong.'

'Maybe,' Kate answered. *Cling to any hope.* That was all you could do.

Kate met the children on their way home from school. She told Harry his mother was unwell, and he was to stay with her for the night. This was not unusual, and he did not object.

After their evening meal, Kate took the children for a walk to the monument on the hill. The warm autumn day was drawing to a close, and the evening breeze was chilled. The sun set into the ocean, the huge golden disk sinking out of sight. The last time she stood on this spot, Michael had wrapped his arms around her to protect her from the world. She missed him. If she closed her eyes tight for a moment, she could sense him. Then she heard the children calling. It was nearly dark – time to go.

Kate opened the front door of Peg's darkened house. The air inside was cold and had a peculiar odour. She closed the door, made her way into the kitchen, drew the curtains, and turned the light on. Peg lay slumped over the table a glass beside her hand, an empty bottle on the table. Kate picked up the bottle and Peg stirred. She lifted her head slowly, squinted her eyes against the light, and rested her chin in her palm.

'Hello, Katey,' Peg said. 'Remembered the sherry, you know what we bought for the Christmas cake. Thought I'd have a little drink to help me sleep.'

Kate held the empty bottle.

'Only had a couple of drinks.' Peg's eyes began to close. 'Sure helps you sleep and then you can't think.'

'Come on, let's get you to bed,' Kate said.

She helped Peg stand. When she tripped on unsteady feet, Kate put her arms around Peg's waist and they made their way to the bedroom.

'Any more sherry? Get us another drink, Katey, sure helps you forget,' Peg said as she struggled into her nightgown.

'It's all gone.'

'Damn.'

'Peg, are you all right?'

'Fine, fine. Why shouldn't I be … my husband's just been killed in this bloody war.'

Peg turned away from Kate and buried her face in the pillow, sobbing, and Kate stroked her tangled blonde hair until she fell asleep again; she pulled the blanket around Peg, locked the door, took the key and went home.

Kate sat at her kitchen table; the younger children were in bed asleep. She looked up as Tilly came into the room. Tilly was growing up, her freckles were fading, and her red hair fell in ringlets past her shoulders. But her green eyes lacked the sparkle that a girl of nearly fifteen should have. *She needs to know about her father,* Kate thought. It's the not knowing that's the worst.

Who would tell her about Michael? She had taken his ring, said she would be his wife, but that didn't give her any official status. Joe would know, but they are together. Who would tell her? Would she know? She would know.

***

Matilda O'Brien had been living with Kate for over three years. She was nearly twelve when she came to live with her and never got used to calling her Aunty. She wanted Kate to let her grow up, go to work, help out. But Kate made her promise to stay at school one more year. It seemed important to Kate, so she had given up arguing about it. Now she stood beside the kitchen table and shook Kate's arm.

'Kate, Kate, are you all right?' Kate was pale, her eyes staring at the wall; she didn't seem to be breathing. Matilda was afraid. 'Kate?'

Kate shook her head and said, 'I'm all right.'

'Shall I make a cup of tea?' Tilly asked.

'That would be nice. I'll just check on Peg first,' Kate said. She pushed herself from the table.

***

Kate opened the door and entered the dark house. Peg was asleep. She returned home, fell into the lounge chair, and took the cup of tea the young woman gave her.

'Did Peg get a telegram?' Tilly asked.

'Yes.'

Tilly sat on the floor beside the couch. 'I'm sorry,' she said.

Kate ran her fingers through the red curls and said, 'Yes.'

She closed her eyes and let the tears run down her cheeks. The young woman took her hand, their sorrow over the death of Billy Kennedy shadowed by the fear they lived with.

Chapter Fourteen

Kate opened the curtains and pushed the windows up to let the sunshine and gentle breeze into Peg's cold house.

Peg stirred and turned over. She dragged her arm across her eyes and said, 'Shut the curtain, Kate.'

Kate drew the curtain and sat on the bed. 'How do you feel?' she asked. She pushed Peg's tangled hair back from her red face.

'Not good.' Her eyes filled with tears. 'It's not fair, Kate, not now, not after all this time.'

'No; it's not.'

'What am I going to do?'

Kate took Peg's hand and said, 'I'll be here.'

'Not if you go away with Michael.' Peg pulled her hand away.

'That won't be for a long time.'

They sat on the bed together, two friends, an invisible wall building between them.

'I have to go shopping. Would you like to come?' Kate asked.

'Not today.'

'Do you need anything?'

'No,' Peg said.

'I'll call in on my way home.'

Peg took Kate's hand and said, 'Please.'

Kate returned home for her purse and ration book. In the High Street, she bought what she could afford of what was available. The autumn sun warmed her body, but she was cold. She decided to call into the church. Perhaps Father O'Reilly could help Peg and perhaps he had news from Frank. She left her string bag in the vestibule and entered the church. Kate blessed herself with the water to her right and then sat in a pew. She felt his presence as he stood beside her and turned to look at him.

'Father?'

'Come outside, Kate,' Morgan O'Reilly said.

Kate stood on legs that didn't want to support her. The priest picked up her shopping bag. She was trembling so much she couldn't stand by the time he sat her on the bench under the gum tree.

'Kate, I have had word. Father Kelly has been hurt. He is returning home. I don't know how serious his injuries are,' he spoke slowly.

'Hurt,' Kate repeated.

'Yes, Kate.'

'Oh, Father.' She bowed her head and tears fell into her lap.

'Mary might know a little more. Have you seen her today?'

Kate shook her head. 'I haven't seen Mary for a while.'

How could this have happened; she was so close to Mary. She had grown up next door. She was the little girl Mary never had, and when Kate and Patrick married, it was so right. Kate told Morgan O'Reilly about Billy Kennedy, and he said he would call on Peg.

'I will talk to Mary as well,' he said.

'So will I, Father,' Kate replied.

Peg's head slumped on the back of the wicker chair; her eyes were closed; she held a glass in her hand. She opened her eyes as Kate walked down the pathway and onto the front veranda.

'G'day, Kate. Did you get your shopping?'

'Where did that come from?' The news about Frank Kelly had pulled the fear Kate lived with into her mind; she was trying to push it away. This didn't help.

'Found it at the bottom of the cupboard. Pour us another drink.'

'No.' Kate took the glass. 'You can't keep doing this.'

'It's just a little drink. I don't feel so bad, it helps.'

'But you can't.'

'It's easy for you to talk,' Peg retorted.

She was unsteady on her feet, and Kate took her arm. Peg pushed her away, saying, 'Go away, Kate, go and leave me alone. Go and wait for your bloody Yankee sailor.'

'Peg?' Kate understood the pain Peg was going through. She understood she was the only one Peg could take her grief out on. It still hurt.

'Leave me alone.'

Kate put the glass on the veranda and stepped onto the pathway.

'Harry?' Peg called.

'I'll look after him. I'll come see you later.'

'Don't,' Peg spat the words at Kate.

Kate went home. She could not face Mary Kelly at the moment, but she must talk to her. She had allowed the silence between them to go on too long; she should talk to her about Michael.

Michael.

He should be home soon; the days had drag when he left. He would normally be gone about six or seven weeks. That was all she knew. It was nearly six weeks since he left.

She put her shopping away, put wood in the bathroom heater, fed the chickens and collected a few eggs. The cutting on Sam's grave stood bare and lifeless in the ground. Maybe her father was right. He said it was too late to take a cutting. She had insisted if she nurtured it and protected it from the weather, it would grow. Maybe it was too late.

Harry slept one more night at Aunty Kate's, but he wanted to go home. When the children were in bed and Tilly sat studying in the front room, Kate went out again. She walked across the dark street onto the veranda and opened the front door. The house was dark and cold, and she ran from room to room, searching. She searched the backyard. No one was home. She returned to her own home, grabbed her cardigan from the back of the kitchen chair, and left a worried girl behind.

Kate stood at the front gate. The cold night air reached through her panic, and she pulled her cardigan together. Where could Peg be? Which way to go? Down the road towards South Terrace seemed right. She hurried. In the half moonlight she saw a figure walking towards her, a woman clutching her arms together. Kate ran.

'Where have you been?' Her panic turned to anger.

'Don't shout, Kate. I've been shopping.'

'Shopping?'

The folded arms held a brown paper bag. Kate snatched the parcel from Peg. She wanted to throw it on the ground, smash the contents, but years of being careful and going without prevented her. She turned and walked back up the road.

'Come back here,' Peg shouted. She caught up to Kate and grabbed her arm to stop her.

'Give it to me.'

Kate turned to face her.

'Give it to me. It's mine.'

'Where did you get it?'

'Billy told me. He always knew where to get a drop. Give it back.'

'You can't keep doing this! What about Harry?'

'You didn't have to wait and wait and wait,' Peg cried. She swung her arms to get the bottle.

Kate stepped away but was unable to avoid the blow; she fell, dropping the parcel. Peg stood looking at the liquid seeping through the brown paper. She saw Kate sitting on the ground, holding her face.

'Kate, are you all right?' Peg stumbled to her knees; tears ran down her cheeks. Kate took her friend's hand; her face hurt, and she didn't think her legs would support her.

'I'm all right.'

'I'm sorry.'

'Come on, let's go home,' Kate said.

Kate let Peg help her up. She took Peg's arm as they walked home and hoped it reassured Peg. It steadied her, she did not feel all right, her head hurt, and she felt ill.

Kate made sure Peg was safe in bed before she returned home and told Tilly to go to bed. She needed time on her own. Her stomach heaved, and she could no longer prevent herself from being sick. She showered and went to bed. As she turned her face into the pillow, she thought, *It wasn't easier for me.* She had loved Patrick Kelly, and when he died, she had cried and wondered how she was going to live without him.

As she drifted to sleep, they were all together. Patrick and Billy chasing two eight-year-old girls up the river embankment. The girls screamed as the boys threatened them with a big jellyfish they carried. On top of the embankment, Frank stood to protect them. This time he was not alone. Another boy watched. He was a little taller with dark brown hair.

Kate woke and found herself crying, tears for Patrick and Frank, tears for Peg and Billy, but Michael. There would be no tears for Michael.

Chapter Fifteen

Kate tried to keep things as normal as possible for Peg. Harry went home, and the children went to school. She shopped with Peg and they talked about Billy and Patrick and Frank. Kate never mentioned Michael.

Morgan O'Reilly called on Peg. On Sunday after Mass, Peg and Harry went home with her mother.

Kate went home with her parents. She was determined to speak to Mary Kelly. She should have spoken to her earlier, not let this happen. The fence had lost a picket years ago, and there had never been any need to replace it. Kate squeezed through the gap. She walked across the lawn, past the vegetable patch, and up the steps to the back veranda. She knocked on the door this time. Mary Kelly opened the door and stood aside to let her in.

'You'd better sit down,' Mary said.

Mary put wood in the kitchen stove and stirred the fire before putting the kettle on top.

Kate sat; she felt queasy. She hadn't felt right since the night she and Peg had fought. Now she felt even worse.

'Why didn't you tell me about Frank?' Kate asked. 'I've had no news from him since he left … you know he expects you to share his letters.'

Mary turned from the stove to face Kate; she did not answer. Kate continued, 'I know you're not happy about Michael. I didn't expect you to be happy. I thought you might understand.'

'Why should I?'

'We love each other,' Kate tried.

'Love,' Mary spat the word at Kate. 'What about Patrick, what about him?'

'He's dead, Mary. He's been dead for four years. I loved him. I always will, but he's dead. What do you …?'

'You didn't love him, Kate. If you had, you wouldn't have thrown yourself at this sailor.'

'That's not true.' Kate rose from the table; she looked Mary in the eyes and said, 'That's not true.'

'And what about Jessie? Will he love her, this sailor of yours? Will he be a father to her, another man's child?'

'He loves Jessie,' Kate said. She knew that.

Mary wrung her hands together and said, 'She's all I've got left. He'll take her away from me. She won't know who I am, where she came from.'

'He wouldn't do that,' Kate said. 'Jessie will always know who you are, where she came from. Michael wouldn't do that.'

Tears ran down Kate's face; she stepped towards her mother-in-law, her friend.

Mary held up her hand and said, 'Go away, Kate. Get out of my home and don't come back. Go to your sailor and leave me alone, and leave my Frank alone too. Don't make trouble for us.'

Kate stared at the anger in Mary Kelly. She tried to understand. Mary had never remarried; she mourned the loss of her husband for all time.

Kate knew Patrick would not have wanted that for her, even if Frank hadn't told her. Patrick loved her, and he would want her to be happy. He would know she had not gone looking for Michael, and she had not thrown herself at him.

There was nothing else to do. She left the kitchen where she'd spent so much of her life; left all the angry words behind.

Kate sat on the swing that hung from the old gum tree in her parent's back yard. She did not see her father approach, and when he spoke, she jumped.

'Come inside and eat,' he said, his Irish accent still there after all these years.

'I'm not hungry.'

'Come on, Kate, your mother's waiting.'

'I understand, dad, I do. She is so angry with me. She wouldn't even listen. Pat wouldn't have wanted me to be like that – he wouldn't.'

She pushed the ground with her feet as she looked at the house next door.

'No, he wouldn't, but Mary can't see that. She sees that you should do what she did,' her father said.

'Maybe if I hadn't met Michael, dad. I hoped she would at least try to understand. How can I take Jessie to see her when she's like that?'

'We'll sort it out. I can take Jessie to see her. Come on now.' Kate could hear the concern in his voice. She had tried to hide her fears and worries from her parents but was not succeeding.

'Come on now.'

'Not yet. Tell mum I'm sorry, I would like to go for a walk. I won't be long.'

'It's all right. Don't go on the beach without your coat; it's getting cold.'

'Yes, Dad.'

Kate ambled along the laneway. The cold wind picked up dust, and she noticed the blue skies of the morning were now grey. She increased her pace and folded her arms against the chill. Kate opened her back gate, walked through the garden, up the steps, and into the cold, empty house. She took her coat from the hook on the back of the front door before opening it. Michael Brannigan stood, his hand raised to knock on the door.

Kate stared, unable to believe her eyes. She dropped her coat, covered her face with her hands, and burst into tears. He wrapped his arms around her, picked her up, pushed the door shut with his foot and carried her into the front room. They sat on the settee, Kate curled in his arms, weeping.

'Not quite the welcome I expected,' he said. 'What's wrong?'

'Sam died,' was all she could say.

She curled close into his body, remembering his scent, his maleness, listening to his heartbeat. If she breathed in deeply, she could even smell the oil from the submarine he lived on.

'It's okay, my darling, it's okay,' he said.

'Okay.' It was Michael – no one else in her world used that word. She missed it, his American drawl; she missed him. Kate wiped her tears away with her fingers and took his face in her hands. His brown eyes smiled and wrinkled up his face. She ran her fingers along the contours of his face; over his cheeks; across his lips; down to the khaki collar of his jacket. He was home, and she said, 'Make love with me, Michael?'

'Now? It's the middle of the day,' he teased.

Kate sat in silk and lace, garments she had kept for best … worn now because her others were tatty and almost beyond repair. She was glad she chose today to wear them. Michael sat on the bed beside her; she helped him remove his shirt, slowly, one button at a time, enjoying his body. She saw the wound on his left arm. Her face went cold.

'It's okay, Kate. It's only a scratch.'

Kate ran her finger lightly down the angry welt from his shoulder to his elbow.

'It's okay,' he said.

He kissed her lips as he slipped the straps of her petticoat down her shoulders. She stood to let her underwear fall to the floor and then she straddled his knees. Kate ran her fingers down his neck, across his shoulders and into the light brown curls on his chest. He lay back; she went to him, pulling him deeply into her. They clung together, bodies entwined, lives woven together, unable and unwilling to be parted.

'You're really here,' Kate said.

'So are you.'

Peaceful sleep came to Kate in Michael's arms.

Michael lay, thinking. The patrol was quiet, their area south of any activity. Towards the end of March, they had received orders about a convoy north of their position. The fuel tanker was an easy target. But the escort ships moved fast. When the tanker went down with its precious cargo, so badly needed, they had pursued the Codfish without mercy. One of the escorts was damaged, but the other two continued the attack; the boat had taken a beating and been badly damaged.

His arm was injured when a steel beam came down. 'Doc' had attended to him as he stood at the pericope, giving Joe details of what was happening above. He felt no pain, which surprised him as he thought he could see the white of his bone. The crew of the Codfish owed their lives to the skill of their Captain. Joe eventually outran the escorts going as deep as they could to hide beneath a layer of extra salty water. Joe had ordered him off the bridge, and 'Doc' had stitched his wound and given him painkillers.

The Codfish limped back to port. The base Doctor removed his stitches, X-rayed his arm, and told him how lucky he was. This he was sure of. He held Kate in his arms. He knew she would be waiting for him, and the real fear he had for her safety seemed rather foolish now he was home. Yes, home. He moved his stiffening arm and pulled Kate close as he closed his eyes to sleep.

He woke first. Kate lay sleeping face down beside him. He kissed her shoulder, and she turned onto her back and opened her eyes.

'How are you?' he asked.

'Oh, Michael, I'm good, really good, even better now.' She put her arms around his neck, pulled him close seeking his body. He gave it willingly.

They lay together, her legs draped over his; she rested her head on his chest.

'How are the girls?' he asked.

'The girls, heavens!' Kate sat up. The bedclothes tangled around her.

'What time is it?'

'Seventeen … sorry, five o'clock.'

'Oh dear, they will be wondering where I am.'

***

Kate sat at the dresser, in grey flannel trousers and a blue floral shirt. *All too old,* she thought. But it wasn't important. She pulled the hairbrush through the tangles in her hair. Her eyes sparkled, her cheeks glowed, and her lips showed a tingle of the colour she had used on them. Michael was home, the waiting over.

Michael returned to the bedroom, buttoning up his jacket. He stood behind her and placed his hands on her shoulders.

'They'll be wondering where I am.'

'They'll know where you have been when we get there.'

'But Michael, they are my parents.'

'Exactly.'

He stood her from the chair; she turned to face him. 'Michael, I love you so much.' She put her arms around his neck, and he lifted her from the ground and kissed her gently on the lips.

'I'm glad of that,' he said, 'really glad.'

***

Jessie Kelly jumped from the swing her grandfather was pushing and ran across the garden as her mother opened the back gate. She remembered 'Tenant Michael, he'd been gone a long time. He was standing with Mummy. Mummy looked very happy but Tilly was behaving very strangely. She ran across the lawn and threw her arms around 'Tenant Michael. Tilly had never done that before. Jessie liked 'Tenant Michael and she let him pick her up and carry her back to Poppy. Poppy looked strange as well.

***

Kate could see her father struggling. Michael put Jessie on the lawn and extended his hand to her father.

'Your mother's been worried,' Sean O'Brien said.

86

'I'm sorry.' Kate lowered her eyes.

'I'm afraid it's my fault, sir,' Michael said. 'Time got away from us.'

'Mmm,' Sean replied. He took the hand Michael offered him.

She was happy; her father had to know that. All he had to do was look at her.

'Mmm,' he repeated.

'I'll see Mum now.'

Kate ran through the garden, up the steps and into the kitchen. Her mother turned from the stove and said, 'Michael's back.'

'Yes.' Kate went into her mother's arms. 'Yes.'

Kate and Michael sat in the dark on an old park bench. It had made its way to her parent's front veranda, battered and unusable until Patrick Kelly had fixed it.

Kate rested her head on his shoulder and listened to him say, 'Joe and I will sleep on board for a few nights. There are repairs to be done. Our crew is having leave, and we hope to have a few days if possible. Will you come to dinner with Joe and me? He would like to see you.'

'I'd like to see him. Bring him home with you,' Kate said.

'He'd like that. We should be there about eight... six o'clock. Is that okay?'

'Yes.'

'I'm sorry I have to leave soon,' he said.

'I understand.' He had his duties to perform.

Kate sat alone on the bench. She had watched Michael walk down the street until he disappeared into the dark. The little port town was going to bed. The dock was only a short walk away, and as the night deepened, the sounds became louder. She could hear them more clearly from her parents' front veranda. The dock never went to sleep.

Her mother opened the front door and said, 'Come inside, love.'

The light from inside fell across the veranda. Once they would never have dared to open a door with a light on. And Kathleen hurried to close it. She sat on the bench, took Kate's hand, and said, 'Come inside. It's getting cold.'

Chapter Sixteen

Kate felt wonderful. Michael was home, and she had slept peacefully all night. She felt a little guilty, but the anxious days had seemed endless, and she was going to enjoy how she felt. He would be home for tea.

It was Monday morning. Once the girls were at school, she had the day to herself. It was time to do her duty with the Red Cross.

The morning sun was cool. Kate walked briskly to warm herself. An old limestone building in Henderson Street had been converted for use by the Red Cross. Ethel Ingram greeted Kate warmly and asked about Billy Kennedy. Kate confirmed the news.

Kate did many tasks at the Red Cross. Rolling bandages, operating tea stands, sorting rags, and visiting the wounded on the ships that were bringing them home.

Today she was to visit the wounded on a hospital ship docked in the harbour. Of all the duties Kate performed for the Red Cross, this was the most unbearable: to see the broken bodies and broken minds of the wounded. She knew her visits and the visits of the other Red Cross volunteers bought joy and comfort to those on the ships. The injured knew they were home and safe when the Red Cross girls visited.

Kate took a deep breath as the ambulance she rode in pulled up at the hospital ship. She walked up the gangway, passed injured bodies being carried on stretchers, passed those who could walk being helped by orderlies, onto the deck of the ship, down into the hull. The smell of disinfectant hung heavy in the air. Her eyes adjusted to the light, and she saw the pain and suffering war causes. She had mail to deliver and letters to read, and she went about her duties.

Kate was reading to a young man, his eyes covered, his arms

limp, reading letters from his mother and girlfriend when she heard her name called.

'Frank,' she answered.

Completing her duty, she called his name again. 'Frank.'

She made her way to him and knelt on the floor beside his bunk. She whispered, 'Frank.'

'Let me see you,' he said.

Kate took his hands and put them to her face. He followed the contours with his fingers; she kissed them as they rested on her lips.

'Don't cry,' he said.

Kate held his hand tight. He lay on a bunk, a thick bandage around his head and eyes, another across his chest.

'Excuse me, Mrs,' a voice behind her said. 'Time to take the Father ashore.'

Kate made sure Frank was comfortable in the ambulance. With the driver waiting for more patients, she said, 'Please wait for me, if you can.'

Kate went in search of the Codfish. She knew where the vessel would be docked. She walked with purpose – anyone who thought to stop her did not, her Red Cross armband giving her an authority she did not have.

It was cold and windy on the dock. The noise pounded her ears. When she reached the quay, the Submarine Tender was tied up, and her path was blocked by a wire fence. There were several submarines tied to the tender. Tied to the dock away from the tender, was the battered hull of a submarine. Men walked about inspecting the damage. Joe and Michael stood on the deck of this vessel, talking.

'Some' damage Michael had said. This didn't look like any submarine she'd seen leaving the harbour. Kate hadn't really thought about how to attract Michael's attention. There was so much noise she would not be heard above it. The wire fence surrounding the pier stopped at a guard post. A gust of wind blew up from the water, lifting her beret and tossing it onto the ground.

She bent to retrieve it and attracted the attention she needed.

Kate ran along the wire fence as Michael hurried along the gangway. They met at the sentry post. Everyone was looking at her now, but Michael was holding her hands tightly.

'What is it?' he asked

'Frank, he's on that ship.' She waved her arms in the direction of the hospital ship. 'He's hurt, he's going to the hospital. I have to go with him.'

'Yes, you do.'

'I don't know when I'll get home.' She tried to keep the tears away.

'It's okay. I'll try and be there.' He brushed her cheeks with his fingers.

'Thank you.' She wanted to hold him, be in his arms but that wouldn't be right, not where they were.

He kissed her gently on the forehead. She watched him return to the battered submarine, *some damage*. Her heart was in bits. She hurried back to the ambulance.

Kate held Frank's hand tightly as she sat beside his bed in the whitewashed hospital ward.

'Well, Lieutenant Kelly,' a voice said.

Kate looked up, squeezed Frank's hand. 'Frank, the doctor's here.'

He stirred.

The doctor said, 'We will have to remove these bandages. I will have you moved to a surgical room.' He called for a wheelchair. 'No more heroics, Father. You are in my hospital and you ride when I say.' He turned to Kate and said, 'Please wait here.'

Kate sat alone in a ward full of injured men. She saw parents comforting their sons, wives reassuring husbands, and men alone and quiet. She couldn't stay there any longer.

On the veranda, the late afternoon sun was shining on a garden full of colour. Tall, robust trees stood in green lawn; flower beds dotted the grounds. 'Don't let him be blind, he doesn't deserve that,' she said to their God.

Frank Kelly sat propped up, a fresh bandage covered his chest and his eyes. Kate sat beside the bed and took his hand.

'Will he be all right?' she asked the doctor who stood beside the bed.

'I can't be sure.' He addressed Frank. 'Your left eye is completely damaged, severely burnt, but you might still have some sight in your right eye. You will have to see someone who knows more than me.'

Kate listened to the mechanical words. As her eyes met the speaker's, she saw it was better not to become too involved. 'The burns on your chest are healing well,' he continued. 'I have given the Father a sedative, he should sleep now. You should go home.' He rested his hand on her shoulder.

'Kate,' Frank said.

'I'm here …' She squeezed his hand.

He ran his fingers around the diamond ring on her left hand.

'Don't fret, I'm home, I'm alive. I'll be fine.'

'Frank …'

'Shush now. How are you and the girls?'

'We are well.' She tried to keep her voice composed.

'And Michael? Is he still at sea?' His words were coming out slowly.

'He came home yesterday.'

'You must go home to him then.'

'Yes, I can go home to Michael now. Good night, dear friend.' She kissed his forehead as he drifted into sleep.

As Kate walked along the hospital veranda Mary Kelly and Morgan O'Reilly came across the darkening lawn. She waited for them on the top step.

'How is he?' Morgan O'Reilly asked.

'He is sleeping. His eyes are damaged,' Kate said.

She looked into Mary's face and the angry words of yesterday – was it only yesterday? – came to her mind. Mary walked past Kate without a word.

Father O'Reilly took Kate's arm and said, 'She's been worried, Kate; try to understand.'

'I am.'

It was dark when Kate arrived home. The girls would go to their grandparents if she wasn't home after school – that was the arrangement, especially on Red Cross day. She did not go straight there; she had to see Michael if it was at all possible, if he was able to get away. Each step seemed ten-foot-high as she climbed onto the veranda. The back door opened, and she fell into the arms of the man she loved.

Kate sat on the settee and rested her head on Michael's shoulder. She held a cup of coffee in her hands.

Michael said, 'I called on your parents and told them what happened. They will keep the girls tonight and send them to school in the morning.'

'Thank you.'

'How is Frank?' he asked.

She sat upright and said, 'He can't see, Michael. He can't see.'

'I'm sorry.'

'He's not even a soldier. He doesn't even carry a weapon. Why did this happen?' She couldn't hide her sorrow, and he pulled her close; she could hear his heart beating.

'I'm sorry, I can't stay. I have to leave soon.'

'I know …' She mumbled his name as her eyes closed. The empty cup fell to the floor and she shook her head, tiredness flooding over her.

'I'm tired.'

She fell asleep in his arms.

Kate dreamed. The men on the hospital ship. Frank Kelly. The battered hull of a submarine. Michael sitting on the bed, his life seeping out of the wound on his arm. He was calling her, crying out for his life, for her life. She woke in terror, alone in her bed, and was unable to prevent herself from being ill before falling back into a fitful sleep.

Chapter Seventeen

Kate woke too late to see the girls to school. The sleepless night made her edgy. She spent her energies cleaning, tidying, and attending to Peg's house. Then she washed her hair and sat on the back step to comb and dry it. The sun warmed her body, and she closed her eyes and turned her face to it.

***

Michael Brannigan came around the side of the house. Kate sat motionless, her eyes closed, her back to the stairs, the sun on her face. His heart sped up; sweat poured from his brow. He froze unable to move his hand to push the wet hair from her still face.

She opened her eyes, and squinted in the sunlight, then wrapped her arms around his neck and asked, 'Is it hot where you live, Michael?'

He sat on the step beside her, calmed the irrational fear that enveloped him, and took her hand.

'Where we will live?'

'Yes.'

He held her hand tighter than he needed, and said, 'New Harbour is lovely. Our old house sits in lawns and overlooks the fishing boats on the water. It's warm in summer, not as hot as here, but it's a bit cold in winter. The apartment in Portland, you won't like. But Pearl is beautiful and warm all the time. It will suit you.'

'Michael?' Kate's face showed how anxious and confused his words had made her.

He had to explain.

'The old house is the family home, Mother's really. I own the apartment. Property is a good investment, and it's in the city near the factory. Mother uses it to run the business. The Navy provides rental accommodation in Pearl, but we can buy a home of our own if you like.'

Turning away from him, Kate tried to hide what he could see.

'It's okay,' he said.

She looked at him and asked, 'Are you off duty now?'

'For a few hours.'

'Let's go for a walk.'

***

Kate couldn't talk to Michael; his words confused her. Her father had insisted on his girls having a High School education. Even during the depression, they were better off than many people. There was always someone earning money in her family's home. When she married Patrick, they were able to pay for their little house. Patrick had made most of their furniture. And they were able to buy a brand-new electric refrigerator. Michael was talking about houses and apartments, and businesses. Things she didn't understand, things people like her didn't have.

'Kate,' he said.

'Let's talk later,' she said.

'Okay.'

Kate could see in his face how reluctant he was to do this. She took his hand and rose from the step. Picking up her old tennis shoes, she tipped them upside down to make sure there were no spiders inside. She straightened up the cardboard lining that covered the hole in the sole then bent to put them on. Remembering words spoken, she said, 'A fine Officer's lady I'll make.'

Kate straightened up in front of him and he said, 'Just fine – all this Officer wants.'

He wrapped his arms around her. All the confusion left her mind and body. In his arms there was no doubt, no confusion, only pure love and happiness; she held onto that. But they must talk; they would be friends as well as lovers.

At the top of the river embankment, Kate and Michael stood in a clearing. They could see the river make its way west, under the bridge, through the harbour, out to the ocean. A gentle breeze did not disturb the clearing. Little black and white birds, with tails that wagged, flew about sipping the nectar from the red bottle-shaped flowers. She loved the green trees that never lost their leaves, the blue sky that went on forever, and the ocean where you could see to the end of the world. Kate leant into his body; he held her tight and said, 'I'm sorry.'

'Don't be sorry,' she said. 'I love you.'

No matter how hard it was going to be to leave her home, it was going to be impossible to stay.

She stared at him with determined eyes. 'I need to be with you. Do you understand?'

'Yes, I do,' he said.

***

Jessica Kelly stood hand in hand with Michael Brannigan in the back garden of her home. The rose cutting that marked where her dead pet lay seemed to be growing. She told him how sad she was when Sam died. Mummy said he had gone to heaven and she wouldn't be able to play with him anymore. She told him that Mummy and Tilly had cried and cried when they put him in the ground, and she had cried too. He picked her up, and she snuggled into his jacket – it was warm and prickly. He carried her inside the house. The kitchen was warm and full of the smells of food cooking. Jessie looked at her mother, she was singing; she didn't remember Mummy singing before. She kissed the cheek of the man who held her.

'Mummy,' Jessie said, 'the rose is growing.'

'Are you sure?' She moved the pot to the side of the stove.

***

Kate hurried out to the back garden. Yes, there was a bud on the stem. She was right; it wasn't too late; the rose had survived. It would sleep now until next spring when it would bud and bloom.

She noticed the chill in the air on the way back to the house and stopped at the wood heap. It was time to light the front room fire. She was struggling up the step when Michael said, 'You should have asked me.'

'I can do it,' she replied.

'Yes, I know.'

So many years … it seemed like so many years. Being alone, doing for herself, she placed the wood in his arms and opened the back door for him. At the hearth, she said, 'I like to light the fire.'

'Okay.'

The thud, and cry, sounded through the house at the same time. Kate sat on the hearth, resting her head on the brick surround. Tilly knelt beside her. Michael and Jessie stood in the doorway of the front room.

'Kate,' Tilly cried.

'Mummy,' Jessie called from the doorway.

'I'm okay.'

Michael helped Kate to her feet and sat her on the settee.

'You okay?'

'Yes, I'm fine just a little dizzy … must have been bending to light the fire.' Kate shook her head to clear the thick feeling; turned to Tilly and said, 'I'm all right, you mustn't fuss.'

She took Jessie by the hand, stood from the settee and said, 'Come on, let's finish in the kitchen.'

Kate smiled at Michael to ease the worry on his face and said, 'I really am all right. Would you light the fire please?'

***

Matilda O'Brien joined Michael Brannigan as he sat on his haunches, lighting the fire. 'Mr Brannigan, Michael …' She never knew what to call him. Jessie called him 'Tenant Michael that didn't seem right for her.

'Michael,' he said as he turned to face her. 'Call me Michael. What is it, Tilly?'

She told him she was worried about Kate, who was so tired. And sometimes when she didn't think anyone was around, she cried. And how Kate had woken in the night crying and been sick.

She said, 'Kate won't tell me if anything is wrong. She still thinks I'm a child. I'll be fifteen soon, I could go to work, help out, but she won't let me.'

Tilly was frightened and could not hide it.

***

Michael put his arm around the young woman. When Kate had turned from the pan she was stirring, he saw how different her life was to his. To what he had grown up with, to what he knew. How different it was, but it was her family and now his. Tilly was part of that family, he tried to ease her worries.

'I'll talk to her, Tilly. I will take care of Kate.' He wanted to say, 'all of you,' but that would have been cruel. So, he repeated. 'I will take care of Kate.'

Michael and Kate sat alone. The girls were in bed, the wireless played quietly in the background. He had to leave soon, but finally he was able to ask her, 'Kate, have you been ill?'

His unreasonable fears made it hard for him to keep his voice calm.

'No, Michael, just a little tired,' she said.

He knew her hidden fears and said, 'You must not worry about me. Nothing's going to happen to me.'

'Yes. I know,' she said.

Then she said, 'Stay here with us when you have leave. Don't go to the hotel. Stay with us.'

He could see how much she needed this, if only he could. 'I can't, Kate, not yet.'

'I don't care what people say, Michael. I really don't.'

'I know.' He knew she really meant what she said. 'We will be married soon. You must see Joe, then we can arrange it.'

A shadow crossed her face and wandered to the corners of her eyes.

'It's only a formality – everyone has to go through it. Come to lunch tomorrow. Joe would like to see you.'

He saw the shadow disappear as she smiled at him and said, 'Yes, I'd like that.'

The watch on his wrist told him he was late, and the car would be waiting out the front.

Chapter Eighteen

Kate was in Joseph Daniels' arms. He had been away from his wife for nearly three years, and she understood his need for female contact. She kissed him on the cheek and then sat beside Michael opposite Joe at a table in the Pier Hotel.

Joe was to interview her and give his consent for her and Michael to marry. It didn't make any difference what he would say, they didn't need that bit of paper to prove their love for each other. It all seemed a bit silly to her: they were grownups, capable of making their own decisions. But it seemed it was something Michael had to do – he had to abide by the same rules as his men. That piece of paper would make her his wife. She would have official status; she would not be left with unanswered questions. She couldn't bear to think what that could mean, and her heart was breaking at the thought of such a thing. She had to move away from this, so she asked. 'Are you having any leave?'

'I will be busy with the repairs,' Joe answered.

Kate turned to Michael, 'Will you be busy too?'

'Yes, but …'

The two men exchanged glances and Kate said, 'What?'

Joe rose from the table, kissed her on the cheek before he joined the other occupants of the room.

Kate and Michael lay in each other's arms in an upstairs room. She lifted her head and said, 'What was that all about?'

He reached for his jacket on the back of the chair and found what he wanted. He held up a set of keys.

'Come away with me?'

'What?'

'One of the maintenance crew has a buddy who owns a hut on the beach. He asked if anyone would like to use it.'

'The girls?'

'Bring them, it's only for a few days. I have to be back on board Monday.'

'Where?'

'Somewhere called Palm Beach. Do you know where it is?'

She nodded yes.

'Well?' he asked.

Kate rolled onto her back, taking the bedclothes with her. Could she? Should she? How different her life was. She caressed his face with her fingers. She would not waste one moment of their precious time together.

'Yes, Michael.' She threw her arms around his neck. 'Yes, yes. When?'

'Tomorrow, if that's okay?'

'Yes.' She would make it okay.

Kate and Michael walked arm in arm along the High Street. Kate greeted those she knew and ignored the hurt when some snubbed her. A shout came from around the corner and people hurried in that direction.

'Come on, Kate. There's coffee at the grocer's,' someone she knew called as they rushed past.

Kate looked at Michael and laughed.

'I'm no good at that,' she said.

On the corner across from the town hall, Kate stopped. A crowd gathered at the grocery store, but her attention was elsewhere.

Kate was looking at a window display in the haberdashery store: civilian clothes, not Land Girls uniforms; not how to make ends meet displays, real civilian clothing, the first she had seen in nearly six years. Maybe all the talk of the war being over soon was right.

One store dummy wore a pair of practical olive-green trousers with a matching woollen jumper. The other was in a dress – a real dress made from white cotton. Pearl buttons ran from the V-shaped neckline down the front to the hem. The collar was embroidered with delicate red roses. The straight sleeves that rested on the elbow had a cuff with matching embroidery. A real dress. What would it be like to buy a real dress?

'Do you like that?' Michael asked.

'Mmm, yes, it's lovely.'

For years, she had patched, cut up and repaired. After Patrick's death she had cut up his trousers to make skirts for the girls; she had run in two pairs for herself. She had used the lining of his suits to make the girls blouses, and his shirts to replace their underwear as they grew. His work clothes she wore in the garden. How nice it would be to go into a shop and buy new things, but even if she had the coupons, she needed her money for other things.

'Would you like that?' Michael asked.

'No. You mustn't.'

***

Michael was amazed by the crowd. It had never been a concern of his, obtaining the necessary items for daily life. His needs were provided for onboard and Amanda Collins was a capable provider in port.

He could buy Kate whatever she needed, but she stubbornly refused to let him help her.

'Kate …' He put his arm around her waist. '… when we are married!'

He was exasperated. He hoped she would relent a little … they would be married soon.

'I can take care of you and the girls … I want too. What difference does a few days make?'

One day if she ever let him, one day they would talk about their future. She must know Joe cares for her and would never stand in the way. What was she afraid of?

'Come on, try it on,' he coaxed.

***

Kate noticed the plural he used when talking about Jessie and Tilly. She loved that, the gentle way he included Tilly in their life. She looked into his serious face.

'Michael, it's been so long. So many years of being careful, going without.' She wasn't complaining, just telling him. 'I can't suddenly have all new things, the war, it wouldn't be right.'

'I can afford it,' he said.

'Once we are married, when everything's approved, then Michael, when everything's approved.'

She felt like a child trying to express something she couldn't quite understand.

The clock on the town hall tower said it was nearly three-twenty.

'It's getting late, the girls will be home soon,' Kate said.

Kate and Michael turned into Solomon Street. Up the road at the corner of Fothergill Street, a group of school children gathered. There were heated words among the group, not audible from where they stood. Two older girls in dark green tunics with white blouses and straw Panama hats left the group tugging a younger girl by the hand. Jessie Kelly shook away the hand that held her and ran down the hilly street.

***

Michael watched the young girl in her green and white checked dress. Her light brown curls, just long enough for her mother to braid, sat on the white collar of her school uniform. She held her straw hat in one hand and her satchel in the other as she ran towards them. His daughter, far away, would she even know who he was let alone love him.

'She will love you, Michael.' Kate held his arm tightly.

'Are you sure?'

'Yes, Michael. You are her father, she must miss you terribly, and she will love you.'

Jessie ran into her mother's open arms and kissed her. She

reached up to Michael and he lifted her from the ground. He held her gently before kissing her cheek; then he set her back on her feet. The two older girls were talking at the front gate. Tilly's friend left, and she hurried inside as Kate and Michael approached.

***

Kate and Tilly walked along the riverbank, autumn weather blowing around them. The sky was beginning to go grey as the sun moved west. Jessie had responded to the plans of a few days away as Kate had hoped, but Tilly was moody and almost hostile. As Michael and Jessie walked ahead looking for shells, Kate decided it was time to talk to her.

'Kate,' Tilly asked, 'What's a whore?'

'Where did you hear that word?'

'Nowhere … at school.' Tilly turned her head away.

'Why do you want to know?' Kate kept her voice calm.

'I don't know what it means.' She turned to look at Kate.

They stopped walking, and Kate said, 'A whore is another name for a prostitute, Tilly. You know how we talked about men and women meeting and falling in love and getting married and how babies are made. Well, a prostitute, or whore as some people say, is a woman who has physical contact with a man, and he pays her money. There is no love between them. They don't want to make babies. They don't live together, and they don't get married.'

Tilly was taller than Kate, and her green eyes told Kate she had lied about how she had heard the word. Kate told her what she thought she needed to know.

Then she asked, 'Why are you and your friends using such words?'

'May's brother said …' Tilly could not hide her anxiety over the question. 'No reason,' she stumbled over her words.

'I love you, Kate.' Tilly said and put her arm around Kate.

Kate kissed her forehead and said, 'And I you.' Then she said, 'Come on, let's catch up to those two.'

Chapter Nineteen

Kate sat opposite her mother as they shared an early morning cup of tea.

'Kate, you can't, for goodness sake. Have you lost your common sense?' her mother said. 'What about the girls?'

'We are all going together. They can miss a few days of school. We are leaving soon. So, you see, we will have a chaperone – two actually.'

It was no use pretending she was concerned because she wasn't. She was going away with Michael, and she didn't care what anyone said. She knew her mum would come around, but she was glad her father was at work. That could wait.

'Don't be angry, Mum. There is so little time.' She took her mother's hand across the kitchen table.

'Yes, I know. Have you thought this through? Are you being careful? What if you were to get pregnant?'

'How, Mum?'

Kate saw her mother's startled look at her words.

'You might, Kate.'

'I don't think so.' Kate tried to lighten her tone.

'Have you told Michael?'

Kate shook her head.

'You must.'

'I know. I should have told him before. I shouldn't have …' Kate looked at the diamond ring on her finger.

'Do you think it would make any difference to him?'

Kate shrugged.

'Would it make any difference to you?'

'No, no, I'm afraid. I just want to be together, not tempt fate, not think too far ahead.' Kate shook her head.

'He wants too?' Kathleen asked.

Kate nodded.

'You must tell him. It might be important to him.'

'I know.' Kate played with the ring on her finger. 'When we are away, I'll talk to him then.'

'Will you be back for Tilly's birthday? Iris and George are bringing the children. And Ruth wrote to say she hoped to come home for the weekend.'

'We will be back on Sunday.'

The taxi ride followed the coast. Jessie knelt on the back seat looking out the rear window at the barbed wire-covered coast that was not accessible to civilians. The island to the south-west protected the bay and kept the waters calm.

The vehicle pulled up in front of a little wooden structure that sat in the sand on the beachfront. The girls jumped out and ran down to the water's edge. Michael paid the driver and made arrangement for their return journey.

Kate's rumbling stomach told her it was time to eat. The front veranda provided a perfect place to share the picnic she'd prepared. The autumn sunshine was warm, and the wind did not disturb the water in front of the house.

Inside the building was simple. Three rooms, one a living area with a wood stove and sink at one end and a fireplace near the front entrance, the two other rooms were for sleeping. The bathroom was out the back. Water was supplied from a rain tank, but there was electricity for lights.

Michael placed the bags in the bedrooms. Kate and the girls in the room with four single beds and his duffle bag in the room with the double bed.

Michael stood at the door as Kate unpacked her bag. He said, 'I've got something for you.' He had his hands behind his back and a smile on his face. 'I won't give it to you if you scold.'

'I won't scold,' she said.

He handed her a brown paper parcel, and she sat on the bed and opened it. Folded inside was the sensible and practical green trousers and matching jumper from the store window. She picked up the jumper and the impractical white dress fell onto her lap.

'Michael,' she whispered.

She stood before the mirrored robe door and held the dress in front of her.

'It's beautiful.' She turned to show him.

'Yes.'

'Thank you.' She would not scold; she did understand.

The front door crashed open.

'Mummy, Mummy, where are you?'

'Here.'

Kate folded the dress and placed it in her suitcase before leaving the room.

'Look, Mummy, look!' Jessie held up a hand full of coloured shells. 'Aren't they pretty?'

'Yes, they are. Why don't you put them out the back to dry.'

Jessie slammed the back door behind her.

At the wood stove, Kate said, 'Let's get this going and make a cup of tea.'

'A cup of tea,' Michael teased.

Kate filled the kettle with water from the rainwater tank out the back and returned to the kitchen to find Michael struggling with the stove. She took the poker from him and soon had the fire burning and the kettle boiling.

The rest of the day was spent walking on the beach, holding hands, the girls ahead or behind them. Michael dressed in khaki so they wouldn't attract too much attention. If they had bothered to look, they would have noticed only kind curiosity. The people of this small coastal community were used to seeing American servicemen as a recreation base was established out at Long Point.

Although this situation was different from what they usually saw. Tilly had her Box Brownie camera with her and took pictures with the few precious bits of film she had. As they walked together, they had the offer of a *family* picture by a stranger who took Tilly's camera and insisted she be part of the photograph.

After the evening meal as the sun set, Michael lit the fire in the living area, and Kate helped the girls bath. The wood chip heater roared and spluttered, and she was glad Patrick had removed the one from her home. She had loved Patrick. Mary was wrong.

It had surprised Kate the way Jessie had taken to Michael. She slept curled up on his knee as they sat in front of the fire. Kate knew he missed his children, his daughter growing up so far away and his little boy, gone now. Jessie had helped fill a gap in his life and was a comfort to him. He would be a good father to her: he would always let her be who she was. It was distressing that Mary thought otherwise.

***

Michael sat on one of the chairs beside the burning fire, Jessie curled up on his knee. She stirred and made herself comfortable, and he pushed her brown curls from her face. His daughter was about this age when he had last seen her. They were so different: Karen was tall and thin, with blue eyes, and straight blonde hair that was almost white. Jessie had the darkest brown eyes he had ever seen, her skin was tanned, and she had freckles on her nose. Kate was combing the older girl's hair by the fire. He wished Karen could meet her. He knew it would be hard for Karen to accept someone in her mother's place, he also knew Kate would love Karen just as he loved Jessie.

It was time for bed.

Michael woke early. The flimsy curtains let the light in. Magpies warbled, sea birds squawked, and the ocean lapped gently on the shore. Quiet, natural sounds woke him — men clambering, and engines throbbing helped him sleep. He dressed in shorts and a sweatshirt and pulled his old college jumper over his head for warmth before he left the room.

He stopped at the door of the other room. Kate was asleep, Jessie curled in her arms; the blankets had fallen off the bed. His love for her wrapped itself around him. He could almost touch and hold it, which he found rather strange and disturbing. He pulled the blanket around her shoulders and she stirred.

'What's wrong?' she mumbled.

'Nothing. It's early, go back to sleep.'

Nothing was wrong; everything was right. How much would he have missed if he hadn't taken the chance to get to know Kate. If he did not have what they now shared, his life would be so different. Because of her, he could share with his daughter her memories of her mother and brother. He hoped Carol would understand. He was faithful to her, never looking for anyone else, prepared to live his life on his own. He never expected to love again, especially not like this. He had not gone looking for Kate, it was as if she was waiting for him, maybe they were waiting for each other.

He found the bakers shop and bought bread and then went looking for milk. The newspaper did not arrive from the city until later in the afternoon he was informed. He made his way back to the cabin and was attempting to light the kitchen stove when Kate woke. She came into the room, closed the bedroom door behind her. Running her hands through her hair, she said, 'Good morning.'

He gave up on the stove and took her in his arms.

'Good morning,' he said and kissed her, holding her tight. He released her when they heard voices from the bedroom.

'Let me help you with that,' she said.

'Yes.'

Friday and Saturday were the days they had to share before returning to wartime worrying. Friday was spent fishing for dinner – the fish were not in any danger – and swimming in water that was too cold to swim in. Michael returned the milk pitcher he had borrowed from the shop and bought candy for the two girls who accompanied him. They ate in the one little café on the seafront, enjoying the quiet seaside town.

Kate and Michael slept in separate beds, cold and lonely, but that was how it had to be.

On Saturday morning Michael took Jessie fishing. He had promised that if she got up early, he would, and so they were up early.

***

Kate and Tilly tidied the house then sat on the veranda step overlooking the ocean. It was still warm, the last of the autumn warmth, in a clear blue sky. Tilly was quiet, and Kate was concerned.

'What's the matter?' she asked.

'Nothing,' the girl answered.

Kate put her arm around Tilly's shoulder. 'Come on, what's wrong?'

'Will Daddy come home, Kate?' She could not hide the tears that fell.

'Yes, Tilly, Daddy will come home.'

'What if he doesn't, Kate. What will happen to me?' She looked out over the ocean.

'If he doesn't,' Kate said firmly, 'I will look after you.'

'But when you marry Mr Brannigan … Michael … what will happen to me then?'

Fifteen tomorrow, it should be the best time of your life, not this.

'I will look after you. Michael knows that, Tilly. You like him, don't you?'

***

Matilda O'Brien did like Michael. He was a nice man, and he said he would take care of Kate when she had talked to him. Kate seemed well and happy now he was home. He was always kind to her, and she knew Jessie loved him. He was a nice man, no matter what some of the kids at school said. They didn't know him, and neither did their parents.

'Yes,' she said.

'Michael likes you,' Kate said. She wiped the tears from Tilly's cheeks. 'Anyway, Daddy will come home.' She kept her voice firm and even.

'Yes,' Matilda said.

A cry from up near the jetty caught their attention, Jessie and Michael were walking towards them.

'Come on. Let's see if we have fish to eat.'

They did not.

***

Kate and Michael walked alone on the sandy shore. Shadows flew across the ground as clouds blocked the sun. It was time to talk.

She kicked her shoes off, rolled up her grey trouser legs and stood ankle-deep in water.

'You'll catch a cold,' Michael said.

She came out of the water and faced him, her feet were frozen, but she said. 'No, I won't. 'I'm one of the O'Brien kids, and we're tough.' That silly old chant from her childhood.

'You never had any brothers or sisters?' she asked.

'No. I had lots of cousins, and I had Amy.'

'Amy?'

***

Michael thought *She's not going to like this.*

Kate said, 'I'm sorry. It's none of my business.'

'Yes, it is. Amy is Benjamin's daughter. We grew up together.'

What words could he use that would not offend her? There were none. He said, 'Benjamin and Meg's daughter. Ben is mother's driver, handyman, gardener, and Meg keeps the house.'

Kate turned and walked away from him. He caught her by the arm, stopped her progress; turned her to face him and said, 'I love

112

you, Kate. Why won't you let me love you like you love me?'

Something was wrong. He knew she wouldn't like what he had told her, but there was something … … the shadows that had been in her eyes since his return. He looked there for his answer.

'Look at me, Michael. I can't fit into a world with drivers and housekeepers. We come from different worlds. I have holes in my shoes; I worked in a dress shop; Patrick was a carpenter. We are the drivers and housekeepers. We don't have housekeepers, gardeners, summer houses, townhouses.'

He pulled her close and kissed her mouth, stopping her words.

'That's not fair.'

'What does it matter, Kate? We used to be the drivers and the gardeners not so long ago. Things worked out for us. I'm comfortable, and I want to share my life with you. Please.'

She took a deep breath and said, 'There is something I have to tell you.'

Now he could see it in her eyes. She sat on the sand, and he sat beside her.

'We haven't used any birth control,' she said.

What was she telling him? … all their lovemaking, he had used no condoms. After all, he'd told his crew, lecturing them before every leave, telling them how and when to use them; telling the crew to make sure they carried some and use it if the need arose.

He had taken so much for granted. But she shouldn't be so upset; she should know he would be happy with such news. He knew a little about her religion – it was the one his cousins belonged too. He hadn't been bought up like them and had sometimes wondered about that. As they grew older, he saw it as such a harsh and unforgiving religion, especially for the girls. He knew what this religion thought about pregnancy out of marriage; maybe he had presumed too much. He would soon put that right; she should know that.

'Tell me,' he said.

'I'm sorry. I'm sorry,' she cried.

'What, Kate?' He was getting worried.

She took another deep breath and continued. 'Michael, after Jessie was born, I had some woman troubles. The doctor said not to worry, so I didn't, but after Pat went away, I thought I was pregnant and went to see him. I was not, but he sent me to see a specialist, it was all very upsetting. Having Jessie caused some damage, and he said I would never have any more children.'

'Never?'

'I had no right to take your ring … please forgive me.'

How could she think that! How could she not understand what she meant to him?

She began tugging at the ring he'd put on her finger.

'Don't!' He grabbed her hands. 'Don't do that. I love you. It would be nice to have a child of our own, but I love you – you are what I want. We have our girls and each other – that is all I need, Kate. Let me love you.'

Kate leant into his body, folded her arms into his chest. He held her tight, knowing that she loved him. And he needed her to understand his love for her. He had never given any thought to having children of their own.

Saturday night the little seaside town filled with servicemen from Long Point. The picture show was on in the evening. Michael dressed in his khaki uniform; he was an Officer and could not be out of uniform with so many men in town. With Kate and the girls, he enjoyed a meal in the little café before walking along the darkening beach back to the small house.

The wind was blowing, darkness surrounded the house. The girls were in the bedroom, Jessie asleep and Tilly writing letters.

Michael sat with Kate in front of the fire, talking. He told her he would be able to bring her home to see her family. Or her parents could come and visit them. He saw the uncertainty these words caused her.

It was time to tell her.

He said, 'Father was in the Navy, but mother and I inherited the business her family ran. It is a very successful business. There is also something else you should know.'

She sat up at his different tone and faced him.

'The family business is boot-making. Mother wanted to help with the war effort, but she is a shrewd businesswoman. She had a chance at a government contract, and she took it.'

Kate glanced at the ring on her finger, he covered it with his hand and said, 'I only ever spent my own money on you. Mother and I argued about the contract. I told her we couldn't profit from the war. I told her she would have to find something to do with the money from the contract. I said we couldn't keep the money in the family. I wanted none of it. So, you might end up with a poor sailor after all.'

'You are all I want.'

He caressed her cheek. 'I must see Joe tomorrow. I want us to be married while we are in port.'

'There is no rush.'

'I know, but I want you to be my wife.'

He needed her to be his wife; he needed to know that she would not have the endless, unanswered waiting if anything happened to him. He needed to know that she would be his wife and would have to be informed and looked after.

How would she manage with that? Did he have a right to put her through that? But it was already too late for that question.

Chapter Twenty

Sunday morning was dull and blustery. Kate and the girls attended Mass in the small chapel by the water before sharing breakfast and gifts with Tilly. Kate had saved coupons and money to buy her a new cardigan. And Michael was able to find her a roll of film for her Box Brownie.

A car horn told them it was time to leave, to return to wartime worrying and waiting, fear and frustration. Michael ensured windows and doors were locked. He had tried to pay for the use of the house, but the owner refused to take his money. On the top shelf of the kitchen cupboard he placed a bottle of the best whisky he was able to find.

The girls carried the bags to the taxi. Kate and Michael stood alone, holding each other, away from the world for just a little longer. Rain began spitting on the car windows as they drove through the main street of the seaside town.

Sunday lunchtime, a taxi pulled up at the gate of a little weatherboard house. Two girls jumped from the vehicle and ran calling to their grandparents, who stood on the front veranda. Family spilled out of the front door calling greetings to the girls.

***

Kate stood at the gate, waiting for Michael as he made arrangements with the driver. He squeezed her hand as they walked through the gate and down the path. On the veranda, they were surrounded by her family, making introductions, hugging and kissing – her older sister, Iris, and her husband, George, their children – her younger sister, Ruth. The children, excited and loud, ran into the house; the adults followed. Then Kate and Michael were alone on the front veranda with Sean and Kathleen O'Brien, her parents. Kate usually got her way with her father, maybe not this time. She looked him straight in the eyes. She wanted his approval, but if she didn't have it, nothing would change how she felt about the man holding her hand.

***

Kathleen O'Brien took her husband's arm and said, 'Dinner is ready.'

Sean had been so angry when she told him Kate was going away with Michael. He had stormed around the house, demanding to know what Michael thought he was doing, demanding to know what had happened to his sensible girl. She had managed to calm him down, but she knew his anger still simmered.

Kathleen wanted nothing to spoil Tilly's birthday. Her father was missing for over three years. She wanted this day to be as special as it could be for Tilly. Michael was standing up to Sean. Kate was radiant, like a beautiful flower that was in the wrong place in the garden. Now it was in the sunshine and flourishing. She saw her husband let the anger slip from his face. A smile began to form on his lips; he patted her hand as they went into the house.

Kathleen stood with Michael in a park, where tall gum trees reached into grey skies that threatened rain. She watched him as he watched Kate with her older sister: two little girls being pushed on a swing by their mothers. Then he saw Kate's father kicking an oval-shaped ball for the two young boys. The boys dived on the ball, one of them yelling 'in the back, Pop! He pushed me in the back! My free-kick'. Kate's brother-in-law pulling the two tumbling boys apart. The younger sister kicking another oval-shaped ball with Tilly. Kathleen saw him understand how much Kate was giving up for him.

'She loves you, Michael,' Kathleen said.

'It will hurt her to leave you,' he said.

'Yes, it will, but it would hurt her more to stay.' Kathleen had grown old without her mother, her parents having died without her

117

being able to say goodbye. Her children had grown up without their grandparents. How much they had all missed. Maybe in the future travel would be easier. Maybe goodbye would not be forever.

'I will look after her,' he said. 'I will look after them all.'

They both looked at the red-haired girl kicking the football. There was no need for words.

Then he said, 'I have the means to bring Kate home for visits. I will do that. You will see them again. I will not take them away from you forever.'

Kathleen put her arm around Michael's waist, and he bent his head and kissed her on the cheek.

∗∗∗

Michael had to leave. It was late Sunday night and the girls were in bed asleep. He leant over Kate on the settee, and she put her arms around his neck and said, 'Please don't leave me tonight.'

The rain was getting heavier, the patter on the roof now a loud drumming. It was late – he could leave before the sun was up. One more night. Tomorrow would be time enough for worrying about neighbours and gossip.

'I won't leave you tonight,' he said.

Chapter Twenty-one

Kate straightened up from the garden and shielded her eyes from the morning sun. A car entered the street; stopped at her gate. Michael opened the door; hurdled the gate and stood before her, grinning. He picked her up, spun her around and held her tight. Then he put her down and held her at arm's length. Excitement sparkled in his eyes.

'Joe's going home,' he said.

'Yes?'

'He's recommended me for Captain of the Codfish. My own command! I'll have my own boat, after all this time.' His brown eyes misted over. 'Because of you.'

'No, Michael,' she said. 'You deserve this, not because of me.'

How much it meant to him … what did it mean to her. He grinned at her, touched his hat and said, 'The Captain's wife you'll be, ma'am. Because I love you.'

He pulled her close and kissed her passionately, on the street, in front of her neighbours. He was all that mattered: she enjoyed kissing him, tasting him, being part of him.

He released his embrace. 'I have to go … can't be late. I'll see you tonight.'

She walked him back to the car and watched as it drove down the road and around the corner. As she turned to go back to her garden, she saw a figure walking up the road.

Kate went to meet Peg. Neighbours stopped their conversation as she passed – that was how it was with people she had known for many years. She quickened her pace to be away from them. Kate greeted her friend and took a bag.

'Michael's home?' Peg Kennedy asked.

'Yes.'

Kate hadn't forgotten about her friend's sorrow. For a few brief days, she had pushed all the unhappy events away.

Two friends shared a cup of tea in Kate's kitchen. Conversation had never been hard between them, but their relationship was changing faster than they realised.

'Have you told Harry?' Kate asked.

'Not yet,' Peg answered. 'I don't know how to tell him.'

'He must be wondering what's happening,' Kate said. 'Is he at school?'

'I dropped him off on the way home. I keep hoping it's not true.'

'I know.'

A knock sounded on the front door. It was nine-thirty. No-one knocked on the door – they just came around the back and inside. Another knock, and Kate went to answer it. She was surprised to see a young American sailor, hat in hand, standing there.

'Mrs Kelly?' he asked.

'Yes.'

He handed her an envelope, which she opened and read.

> *My dear Kate,*
> *Could you meet me at the hotel at 12.30. I will send a*
> *car for you.*
>
> *Joseph Daniels.*

'Everything all right?' Peg asked.

'Yes.'

'I'd better go.'

The young man stood aside for Peg.

'Excuse me, ma'am. Is there an answer? Captain Daniels said I was to bring an answer.'

'Yes, of course.' Why would Joe send such an invitation? 'Tell Captain Daniels I will join him, but there is no need to send a car.'

Kate stood in front of the mirror. She had changed into the

trousers and jumper Michael had given her and was pleased with how she looked. Her hair was pushed behind her ears, rolled under and held in place with a snood net – the olive-green set off her blue eyes. Kate patted excess colour from her lips. She had promised Michael she would see the doctor, after all the fuss he'd made when she'd dropped the wood. She knew it was a waste of time, but if she hurried, it could be done before meeting Joe.

'Well, Kate?' Dr Joshua Fredericks asked when she'd sat on the other side of his desk, 'what can I do for you?'

She told him she was a little dizzy and sometimes overly tired and unwell. She felt perfectly fine now, but at the insistence of her family, she had come to see him.

He looked up from his notes and asked, 'When did you last menstruate, Kate?'

'Heavens,' Kate reeled, surprised by his question. 'December or January.'

'Didn't you think that was odd?'

'No. It happened when I was worried about Pat. You said it sometimes happens like that.'

'Ahh. Have you been having intercourse?'

'Yes, but you said …' Kate grew flustered; her cheeks were burning.

'I know, I said it would be very unlikely that you could get pregnant and I'm probably wrong. Let's have a look at you.'

Kate's fingers were clumsy as she dressed, then she sat in front of the desk again.

'Well,' he said. 'I would say you are about ten weeks pregnant. Would that be right? Were you having intercourse in the first or second week of February?'

'Yes,' Kate mumbled.

Yes, yes, yes. She was pregnant! *Michael's baby. Michael's baby.*

'Kate,' he said, 'do you remember what else I said after you had Jessie. It will not be easy for you to have this baby – you do not have to go through with this pregnancy.'

What is he saying? … Michael's baby … not go through with the pregnancy … what is he talking about?

'No,' she cried and folded her arms across her stomach.

'Kate!'

'No. Everything will be all right.'

'Do you remember having Jessie? Do you remember how difficult that was?'

'No. I must have this baby … surely there are ways.'

'There are ways to help, and we can never be a hundred per cent sure or we wouldn't be having this conversation.'

'It will be okay,' Kate said. *'Okay?'*

'All right, all right. Do you still see the father?'

'Of course. We are to be married.' Kate was offended. How could he think that? He'd known her since childhood; he'd gone to high school with her brother and Frank Kelly. The boys had all grown up together.

'He has a right to know the risks involved.'

'Michael, no!' Kate knew what Michael would say if he thought there was any risk to her.

She would tell Michael the good news. Joshua Fredericks was making such a fuss. He'd sent her off to the specialist; had all those tests done, all the poking and prodding and they were wrong. She was pregnant, a baby conceived in such love must be born. He would never cause her any harm. *'He'*, she smiled to herself and then at the worried man across the table.

'Everything will be all right,' she said.

He began writing as he said, 'I have issued you with extra milk rations. Make sure you drink it yourself. Come and see me in about three weeks. Sooner if you want.' He stood from his desk and walked her to the door.

Chapter Twenty-two

Kate danced along the street. *Michael's baby, his baby.* He said it didn't matter if they could not have their own child and she believed him. If it didn't matter, why was she so happy? Heads turned as she skipped up the steps and pushed the door of the Pier Hotel opened. She came to an abrupt halt as Joseph Daniels stood to greet her. He was not alone.

Joseph Daniels took her hand. She couldn't hide the joy at the news she had just received. She could see the query in his eyes.

He said, 'I'm glad you came.'

'Yes.' Kate saw the strangers with Joe.

He introduced the two men. Commodore Hale was a stocky man, his dark hair going grey, his khaki jacket pulled at its buttons. He had a gentle, round, lined face and a pleasant smile. Steven Jacobs was thin and hard. His face bore no smile, and his cold, pale blue eyes looked Kate up and down, making her feel uncomfortable.

'Kate, have you seen Michael today?' Joe asked.

'Yes.'

'So you know about the boat?'

'Yes.'

'Because of that it has become necessary for you to talk to Commodore Hale,' Joe said.

Kate turned to the older man, but it was the other one that spoke.

'Mrs Kelly, your maiden name was O'Brien. You came to this country when you were a baby. You were taught by the Nuns at the convent. And you worked in a dress shop before you married Patrick Kelly. You have a daughter, six years old, and you are bringing up your brother's child. She is fourteen years old.'

'Fifteen,' was all Kate could say.

The contempt in his voice startled her. He made her life sound like a collection of distasteful facts. Surely Michael hadn't been questioned in such detail about her.

'Your husband was a member of the Communist Party?'

Michael didn't know anything about this.

She turned to Steven Jacobs and said, 'My husband is dead.'

'He was a member of the Communist Party?'

Kate heard the rise in his tone. 'He wasn't a member.' She kept her voice quiet and steady.

'He was involved with them?'

'Yes.'

'You were not?'

How did he know all this? What business of his was it? 'No,' she said.

'Why not, Mrs Kelly, I thought the duty of a wife was to support her husband?'

He was making a point, almost gloating. Kate was angry. Patrick was a good man, and he had nothing to do with this horrible man sitting opposite her.

'Why don't you tell me? You seem to know everything about me,' Kate struggled to keep her voice even.

The smile from across the table made Kate shudder; she moved her chair to leave. Joseph Daniels placed his hand over hers. It helped her calm down and retain her seat. The man opposite her glared at Joe.

Kate sat straight. She looked Steven Jacobs in the eyes and said, 'Patrick never told me what to think. He wanted me to have my own opinions, and I wouldn't expect it to be any other way.'

Kate could tell he wasn't interested in what she was saying. She didn't what to talk to him anymore. But it was important, so she asked him, 'Have you ever been hungry, Mr Jacobs? I mean really hungry and not known where your next meal might come from? I haven't, but Patrick had. His mother was proud – stupid sometimes

– she wouldn't take charity. We all helped out, no one starved, but bad food and lack of medicine caused the death of a close friend.'

Kate was getting unsettled, losing her composure; she didn't want to do that. Taking a calming breath, she said, 'Patrick was young, he went to a few meetings. I didn't. I didn't like many of the things the party stood for. Patrick thought the Communist Party might give everyone a fair go. Enough to eat, good medicine and a roof over their head.'

Kate was suddenly tired. 'It was a long time ago. Why does it matter?' she asked.

'If you marry Lieutenant Brannigan and if he takes command of the Codfish, your past …'

Kate wasn't listening anymore. He said *if*. *If* he takes command. Michael was so happy this morning: *his* boat, *his* command. It was so important to him. She had nothing more to say to the man opposite.

He was going on: 'It is normal policy when servicemen want to marry local girls to defer the approval for six months. There is no reason why Lieutenant Brannigan should have to marry you now, is there?'

'Mr Jacobs!' Commodore Hale spoke.

'Michael doesn't have to marry me …' She turned to speak to the Commodore. 'May I ask you something?'

'Yes.'

'You love your wife?'

'Of course.'

'I love Michael … Lieutenant Brannigan … but he must have this command. If something that happened all those years ago matters so much, I will not stand in his way. If it means we don't marry, then we don't.'

There was nothing else to say. She could not believe the words she'd said, but knew they were true. She turned her head and looked out the window.

'Thank you, Mrs Kelly,' the Commodore said. He turned to

Jacobs and said, 'We are finished here.' To Joe, he said. 'Please come and see me at 16.00 hours today.'

Joe Daniels stood as his senior officer left the table. Kate stayed seated. She didn't know what was expected of her; there was so much she didn't know.

'Can I get you a cup of coffee?' Joe asked when they were alone.

'I'd like to go home.' Kate pushed herself from the table, her chair scraping along the floor. The room swayed around her and she closed her eyes as her knees gave way.

Joe wrapped her in his arms and helped her to the settee near the fire.

'You're pregnant, Kate?' Joe asked.

'Yes.'

'That's wonderful.'

'Yes, Joe, it is wonderful, but Michael mustn't know,' she told him.

'Kate, you don't mean that?'

'I do, Joe. Please, he must not know, not yet. He was so happy and proud this morning. His boat … it means so much to him.'

'So do you,' Joe said. 'He has a right to know, Kate.'

'I have my rights too,' she cried.

'Yes, you do.'

He wiped the tears from her cheeks and pulled her close, their friendship so new and so dear to them, pure and innocent. Kate clung to him, causing Amanda Collins to stare from behind the bar where she was wiping glasses. Joe released his embrace, took her face in his hands and said, 'Trust Michael, Kate. Trust him.'

He kissed her forehead and put his arm around her; let her rest on his shoulder – more acceptable behaviour for friends.

Kate sat in front of the kitchen stove. She was ready for bed, her wet hair braided in two plaits down her back. In one day … only one day … she had gone from the heights of happiness to the depths of despair. No, not despair. She could not be unhappy with the precious life she carried. Michael would call if he could, but it was nearly ten o'clock. The back door opened, and she was in his arms, breathing him in, feeling his heartbeat.

His tired eyes shone as he sat at the kitchen table and drank the coffee she poured.

'Did you keep your promise and see the Doctor?' he asked her.

She had hoped he would forget that promise, just for today. She had wonderful, wonderful news if only she could tell him.

She said, 'I did, and he thinks I'm just a little low on iron, and he has given me a tonic to take.'

Not really a lie. She should tell him about lunch and that man Jacobs. Joe would. She also knew Joe would keep her secret.

'How did your day go?' she asked.

'Kate, I've waited so long,' he said.

She held his hand tightly. 'Can you stay tonight?' she asked.

'I'm sorry … I have to stay on board. The repairs are being done quicker than we thought. It should be complete by Friday.'

'Will you leave then?'

'I'm sorry.'

'So soon.'

'We will have to rush our wedding plans,' he said.

Kate could see the cold blue eyes that cut through her, the contempt and hatred. *If,* he'd said. *If.*

'What's wrong, Kate?' Michael asked.

She rose from the table, her arms folded across her stomach. *Your child, Michael, I carry your child.* She wanted to say these words to him. How could she?

He took her trembling arms.

'Hold me, Michael,' she said unnecessarily.

His arms wrapped around her, and she clung to him desperately.

'Okay. What's wrong?' He pushed her gently away.

'We know so little about each other.'

'Kate!'

Frustration showed on his face, and Kate said, 'Patrick was

involved with the Communist Party.'

'And you?' he asked her.

'I wasn't.'

She moved away from him, taking her anxiety and desperation out on him. 'Don't you want to know why? Don't you want to question me?'

'No, I don't want to question you. I'm pleased you weren't involved, I won't deny that. You can tell me if you want.' He took her arms and pulled her close. 'What's wrong?'

'I met with Joe and a Commodore Hale today,' she told him.

'Commodore Hale! I saw him this morning. He will be my commanding officer … he is fair-minded,' he said.

'Yes. I also met a man called Jacobs.' She pulled away from his body.

'He hated me, Michael. He … He hated you, because of me. He won't let you get your command if you marry me.'

'It's not up to him.' He held her arms. 'We will be married.'

'At the expense of losing your command?' It was too much to ask him to give up.

'It won't come to that,' he said.

'What if it does? He knows everything about us. How does he know all that? What about Jessie? Will something Patrick did be held against her? She didn't even know him.'

He held her at arm's length and looked into her eyes, and said calmly, 'I will be her father. Do you have any doubt I can protect her?'

She shook her head. 'I have no doubt.'

She knew he would protect Jessie. He would protect them all. Her body trembled, and her legs felt like jelly. If he hadn't been holding her arms, she would have been on the floor.

***

Michael knew Steven Jacobs only by reputation. He was in the military police and had a known paranoia about communism. Surely his marriage to Kate didn't warrant his attention.

She had to know nothing would stop him from being with her. She really didn't know how much she had given him. He should have had his own command years ago, but after the accident, it seemed so far away. He loved her so much. Why wouldn't she let him love her? What was she afraid of?

'He will destroy you,' Kate said.

He sat her on the kitchen chair and kissed her lightly on the forehead. His hands on her arms were gentle; they showed the strength of his self-control.

'Let him try,' he said and left the room.

***

Kate rested her head on the table. She put her hand on her knee, where her beloved pet would rest his head; ran her fingers through the ruff under his chin.

'Oh, Sam, what are we going to do?' she asked him.

***

Michael Brannigan stormed along the gangway of the submarine Codfish. The ride back from Kate's home seemed to take forever, and he had maintained his calm until he reached the dock. The few crewmen who were aboard this late at night avoided him as he stormed into his Captain's wardroom. The tiny room was crowded, heated words filled the air. He let his frustration override the standard of behaviour expected of him by his Captain as he paced up and down.

'Sit down, Mike,' Joe said.

'Why did you let Jacobs question her? I will marry Kate even if I have to resign!' He raised his voice and slammed his fist into the cabin wall.

'You forget yourself, mister. Come to attention when you address me.'

Michael stood to attention, more than half his life spent obeying rules.

'Now sit down!'

He sat upright.

Joe Daniels said, 'I saw Commodore Hale this afternoon after he met Kate. I told him I would have no hesitation approving your marriage, but it's not up to me. Wait and see what he has to say. Kate won't let you give up your command, you know that.'

He did know that.

'She can't stop me,' he said.

Chapter Twenty-three

Kate tucked the blanket around Frank Kelly's legs where he sat in a wheelchair under a gum tree in the hospital grounds. His wounds were healing, but his eyes were still covered with heavy bandages. The blue sky held no warmth as a cold wind blew in off the ocean.

'What's wrong, Kate?' he asked as he took her hand.

'Can you tell?'

'Kate?'

She should have known better. She thought she was masking her feelings, talking about the usual things people talk about when visiting hospitals – sharing news, being happy. She told him about her meeting with Commodore Hale and Steven Jacobs. She didn't tell him anything else.

'He hated me, Frank. He didn't even know me, and he hated me for something Patrick believed in. Why? How can I live with people like that? He hated Michael because of me. He will ruin his career, take away everything Michael has waited so long for. I can't let him do that.'

'No,' he agreed. 'But Michael will make that decision; you can't stop him.'

'Oh, Frank, maybe God is angry with me. I thought I had reached an agreement with Him. I am not ashamed or guilty about my love for Michael. Maybe He is angry that I have bent the rules. I don't care … for Michael I would do it all again. Maybe this is punishment. Maybe this is hell.'

'Don't, Kate! Don't give up your faith – trust God.'

'I don't know any more. Maybe it is wrong to love someone so much, to give them so much of yourself. I don't think I have that kind of faith anymore.'

'You know the love of a man and woman is sacred to Him,' Frank said.

She looked at his covered eyes, and he said, 'It wasn't God's fault, Kate. He didn't make the war.'

'But He let it happen,' she said.

'Don't give up your faith, Kate,' he repeated.

She knew his greatest love was his God.

Kate arrived home around noon. She made sandwiches and tea and sat pushing the bread around her plate as she drank the warm brew. Everyone was giving her advice, telling her to have faith and trust. Why was it so hard to listen? She could not let Michael give up his command, but how could she stop him, especially when he finds out about the baby. *Our baby.* She put her hand protectively over her stomach.

The back door opened.

''day, Katey.' Peg slurred her words as she leant against the door frame.

'You're drunk.'

Kate stood to help her friend. Peg brushed her away and sat at the table.

'Not yet, Katey, but I'm going to be, you wait and see.'

Kate sat opposite Peg and said, 'Why?' She didn't want this today.

'Why not?'

'Peg, you can't get drunk all the time. It's not right.'

'Not right. Not right! Listen to her ... little miss perfect! You should hear what they say about you, Katey.'

Peg pushed her chair from the table and grabbed Kate by the wrist, wrenching her to her feet. 'Whore! That's what they call you. How about that, whore?'

'Don't, Peg.' Kate tugged at the hands that held her, but she could not escape.

'What's the matter, Katey. Where's your bloody Yankee sailor now?'

'Please, Peg,' Kate cried.

Tears ran down Kate's face. She pulled her hands free and stared at her friend. What was happening to them?

'Don't,' she said.

Peg reached out, but Kate stepped back from her touch. Peg turned and left the kitchen.

Kate fell back onto the kitchen chair, crossed her arms on the table and buried her head in them. She let herself cry.

The sound of her daughter coming up the back step woke Kate. Jessie stopped in the doorway and asked, 'Are you sick, Mummy?'

'Just a little tired.' Kate kissed her child's cheek.

She turned to the kitchen sink to prepare a snack, keeping her face hidden as she washed the tear stains away.

Footsteps sounded around the side of the house; up the step. The back door slammed open, the silence that followed not right.

Kate turned from the sink. His face pale, his eyes darting around the room to find her, Harry Kennedy said, 'Mummy won't wake up.'

'Stay with Jessie. I will go and wake her up.' Kate ran.

'Stay with the children, Tilly,' she told her startled niece, who stood talking to her school friend at the front gate.

Peg was on the kitchen floor, an empty bottle beside her. Blood ran from her forehead. Kate tried to wake her, but Peg didn't stir. She ran up the road to a neighbour who had a telephone and called the hospital.

The ambulance arrived with sirens flashing.

Harry saw his mother being carried on a stretcher and ran, screaming, across the road. Kate struggled to restrain him. She took the children to her parents and explained what she could.

In the hospital waiting room, Kate grabbed the arm of a passing nurse and asked what was happening. She was told the doctor was doing his best and to sit and wait. But Kate couldn't sit any longer and paced up and down the hallway. The hospital smelt; they always smelt. And it was cold. She was cold. She had been waiting for so long, just waiting.

She did not hear the footsteps as they echoed on the floor, but she knew it was Michael who turned her around and pulled her close. He was warm and strong, and she took in his strength, his love, as she put her arms around him. Her eyes stung, and her face was wet from her tears.

'Why?' she cried. She pounded his jacket with her clenched fists. 'Why did she do this?'

Michael took her wrists and held them tight. 'Don't be hard on her, Kate. Sometimes it helps with the pain.'

'I know what it's like,' she cried.

'We all do,' he said.

He looked into her eyes, and she could see into his soul. They clung together, and remembered, blotting out memories, making new ones.

***

Michael pushed her from his grip, and she stood in front of him. He knew she was strong, stronger than she knew – the strength of a woman who stays behind – who doesn't have a uniform to wear – who doesn't have an army to march in – who keeps the home and the children safe. But that strength was like glass and it was cracking. She was fragile and vulnerable.

He stared into her eyes; she held nothing back from him, but she wouldn't let him do the same for her. He needed to love her the same way she loved him. 'Let me love you, Kate … let me love you like you love me,' he said.

'Yes, Michael,' she said. 'Like I love you.' He pulled her into his embrace, and she rested her brow on his chest.

***

Kate stood beside the bed. Peg's eyes were barely open, her

damp blonde hair clinging to her face.

'Will she be all right?' Kate asked the doctor.

'I think so. I've done everything I can.'

'I'm sorry,' Peg mumbled. 'I'm sorry.' She said the words to Kate, but her eyes rested on Michael.

Kate took her hand, 'Everything is all right; it will be all right. Go to sleep and get better. I'll see you tomorrow.'

Kate dropped onto the settee in her parents' lounge. 'She will be all right,' she said.

Michael took his jacket from her shoulders and sat beside her.

'Thank God,' Kathleen said. 'The children are asleep. Harry was very upset.'

'I'll go and talk to him.' Kate pushed herself from the sofa.

'Don't wake him. I'll make us a cup of tea.'

'Perhaps Michael would like something stronger,' Sean O'Brien offered.

'Thank you, sir, but I can't stay. I have to get back to the boat.'

'Come and help me with the tea, Sean,' Kathleen said.

'I'm sorry,' Michael said.

'It's okay.'

She knew he wasn't staying: the taxi was still waiting at the front gate. She tried to stand, and he said, 'Don't come out.'

***

Michael noticed the tiredness that flooded over Kate. He wrapped her in his arms and said, 'I love you, Kate, no matter what happens, I will do what needs to be done.'

He left her sitting on the settee and went into the kitchen to say his goodbyes. Sean O'Brien walked him to the front door. Kate sat with her eyes closed, her head slumped on the back of the settee. He hesitated at the lounge room door. The older man rested his hand on his arm and said, 'You have your duties to attend to. We will look after Kate.'

Chapter Twenty-four

Kate and Michael sat before a dying fire. She did not put more wood on as a black car was waiting at her front gate. Michael would not be staying long.

The trauma of the previous day was beginning to fade as Kate listened to him say: 'We will be married. I love you too much to want a life without you, but I have my duty to my country and my crew. I cannot abandon them while the war continues. When it is over, if things don't go as we plan, I will resign.' He stopped her protests and continued, 'I will make that decision. I have told Commodore Hale what I have told you. I am still taking command of the boat. I will be a good Captain. I have you and our girls and everything is going to be okay.'

'Yes, it will be,' she smiled. It was nice to think how it might be. He had taken charge, and for now, that was all right. She was too tired and frightened to argue with him. The news of the baby would wait.

'We leave on Friday. Will you come and see us off if I can arrange it?'

'Yes …' She kept her voice steady. '… of course, I'll come.'

He was so proud. How could she do anything else?

'I will come and see you tomorrow afternoon. I promise we will have some time together and I must see Jessie and Tilly before I leave.'

Kate stood in the open doorway and watched Michael walk down the path. He opened the car door, sat in the back seat and the car drove away.

The night sky was full of stars. They shone so bright and seemed so close, so much beauty in a world on fire. Kate reached her hand out to touch them. She had to be strong, the precious life she carried deserved the best she could give it. It would be hard, but she was 'tough'. Did that old description still apply to her?

Kate and Michael shared their bodies. She lay with her back pressed into his chest, his arms wrapped around her. Would she ever be in his arms again; ever feel his body next to hers? Would she ever be held like this again?

'I will be okay,' Michael said.

She turned to face him and said simply, 'I love you, Michael.'

He would be okay; there could be no other way. She would not go on living in fear, she was tired of that. She curled into his body, and they slept peacefully together for just a little longer.

***

Jessica Kelly clung tightly to the hand she held. They had walked down the hilly street, passed the railway station, to the dock. The sun had set. The half-light cast by the dusk and the browned-out lighting of the dock was frightening. The noise and dust blew around her legs and she was scared, but that wasn't why she held the hand so tightly. 'Tenant Michael' was leaving, and she didn't want him to go. Tilly said she had to be brave and as he picked her up, she was trying really hard.

'Will you be gone a long time?' Jessie asked.

'A little while,' Michael said.

'Do you get frightened?' she asked.

'Yes,' he said. 'Sometimes I do. I think everyone gets frightened sometimes, don't you?'

'Yes.'

Jessie got frightened. When Mummy was sick, she was frightened. And when Mummy was sad, she was frightened. Maybe that's why she was frightened today. 'I don't want you to go,' she said.

'I know. I'll be back soon.'

'And you will be my daddy then?'

'Yes,' he said. 'I will be your daddy.'

She kissed Michael and held him tightly before slipping to the ground.

***

Matilda O'Brien put her arms around Michael Brannigan. He was always kind to her, and she knew how much Kate and Jessie loved him. He would be a good daddy to Jessie. Kate had said he would look after her, if … …

She shook that thought away and said, 'Come back soon.'

'I will,' he replied and kissed her gently on the cheek.

Tilly took Jessie by the hand and followed the wire fence that surrounded the pier. She had to be grown up and brave. She watched Michael take Kate's hand. Sometimes she had to be more grown-up than Kate.

***

Michael reached inside his jacket pocket and said, 'I have something I want you to have. It was my Grandmother's. She gave it to me before she died; she said one day I would meet the person it belongs to. It is for you.'

He had put his picture and a picture of Kate inside the heart-shaped locket.

'Wear this and I will know you are safe.'

He fastened the clip around her neck and pulled her close. Kate closed her eyes as his lips met hers and kissed her mouth. She put her arms around his waist and pressed her body into his. He could not hold her any tighter without hurting her. He had to let her go and tore himself away. Then he walked through the sentry gate and didn't look back.

***

Kate closed the gold locket, sealing the pictures together. She turned it over and stared at the old letters inscribed on the back.

'Come on, Kate,' Tilly said, taking Kate's arm and guiding her away from the pier, the dock, the noise and the smells.

Kate held Jessie's hand and let Tilly lead her home. Was it possible for Michael's grandmother to have known about her? The letters were still in her eyes: 'Forever.'

Chapter Twenty-five

A taxi called for Kate on Friday 20th April 1945. She met Joseph Daniels at the pier. He escorted her through the sentry post to the wharf where the Codfish was tied up. The warm autumn weather had come to a sudden end. The sky was now grey and heavy clouds threatened rain. The water around the submarine was murky and choppy, and the vessel moved on the swell.

***

Michael Brannigan stood on the bridge, in the conning tower. His executive officer, a young man straight out of the academy and new to the boat, stood beside him. Joseph Daniels had handed over command of the Codfish to him at a small official ceremony earlier in the day, Joe having commanded the Codfish since she was commissioned in the late thirties. She was one of the few remaining from the original fleet. Michael had been second in command for all that time, and he shared Joe's pride in this achievement. She was a good boat, and he would look after her.

He gave orders and directions. The tugs began their task of pushing and pulling the Codfish through the harbour. He turned to the wharf, saluted his Captain and friend and tipped his hat to Kate. Then he turned his attention to tasks that would help end this war, so life could go on.

***

Kate heard Joe whisper. 'Take good care of her, Mike.'

She saw in his eyes what it meant to men like Joe and Michael, their own command, their own boat. She could not take that away from Michael.

'Be safe,' she said.

'They'll be okay,' Joe said. 'She's a good boat, the Codfish. She won't let Michael down. She a tough old girl.' Kate smiled at that.

She stood staring at the empty dock. Steady rain began to fall, wetting her woollen coat, making it heavy. The tugs were returning. Joe put his arm around her and said, 'Let's go now.'

Kate and Joe Daniels shared a cup of tea. She enjoyed his company, as he did hers, and they would always be friends. Michael understood this. But she wondered what Joe's wife would think.

It was time for Joe to leave.

'Joe?' she asked. 'Commodore Hale … did he …?'

'I haven't heard anything, Kate. I'm sure it will be okay.'

'That Jacobs?' She could see his face in her mind.

'It's not up to him.'

'Mmm.'

'Kate, did you tell Michael about the baby?'

She shook her head, no.

'Kate.'

'He had enough on his mind. Once we get permission … Anyway he'll be able to tell when he returns.' She placed her hand over her stomach.

'Kate, it is Michael's child as well.'

'Yes, Joe, I know.'

Kate and Joe stood beside the car at her front gate. The rain had stopped, but the sky was grey and dull.

'May I call on you until I leave?' he asked.

'I would like that. I will miss you when you leave.'

'And I you.'

He took her in his arms and held her tight before kissing her on the cheek – a simple act that would cost her dearly. If she had known, she might have refrained, but it was a natural thing for her to do when saying goodbye to a friend.

She watched the car drive away and saw curtains move in windows. She knew about the gossip but had not realised how vicious it was until that day with Peg. She folded her arms across her stomach, more gossip for them. She wanted to shout it out loud, but other people had a right to know before her neighbours.

Chapter Twenty-six

On Wednesday 25th April, Kate attended the Anzac Day parade with the children. In the evening, she picked the last of Patrick's roses and took them to the memorial on the hill.

Kate ran her fingers along the letters that read P Kelly. Patrick's name was yet to be added.

This was the only place to bring flowers. Patrick's body lay in a desert overseas; she would never be able to take flowers there. His father's body had never been found. The name on the memorial was the only evidence that he had lived, and died. It had been there for over twenty years.

She loved Patrick Kelly, but it was time to say goodbye. She always came with his mother on this special day, but not today. She saw the solitary figure of an older woman walking across the grass. Kate placed her flowers at the foot of the monument along with so many others and hoped that one day Mary Kelly would understand. She loved Michael – Patrick would understand this. Mary could not.

On Friday 27th April, Kate received an invitation. She dressed in her olive trousers and matching top. Her hair was rolled in the snood net, and she'd polished her shoes. Kate applied just enough colour to her cheeks and little lipstick.

The last time she stood on the steps of the Pier Hotel, she was full of wonderful news. Her hand was tentative as she pushed the door open.

He was alone and rose from the table as she approached; he held her chair out for her to sit. Then he sat opposite her and said, 'May I get you a cup of tea?'

'Actually,' she said, 'I would like a cup of coffee.'

A smile brushed his face at her words.

'Thank you for coming, Mrs Kelly,' Commodore Mackenzie Hale said.

'My name is Kate,' she told him.

'Thank you for coming, Kate.'

'Yes.' What did he want?

'First I must apologise for your treatment last time we met.'

She didn't want to trust him.

'How much do you know about Commander Brannigan?' he asked.

'I know what he has told me,' she said.

She trusted Michael completely. There was nothing this man could say to her that would change that.

'Then you know that he has been in the Navy for much of his life. Did you know he was second in his class at the academy?'

She didn't know that.

'Did he tell you he was to take command of his own boat in December 1941?'

'No.'

'He has told you about his wife and child?'

'Of course, he has.' She instinctively placed her hand on her belly. Why? Why had she done that? Maybe he wouldn't notice.

He said, 'The attack on Pearl Harbour shook our nation. We were angry and in shock. One man's grief was easily lost in the turmoil. Captain Daniels knew and stood in the way of this promotion. He was correct. Commander Brannigan is a good officer; he did what we expected of him, but he was in no fit state to take command of his own boat.'

Kate nodded.

'We have given him command of the Codfish. We believe he is ready to do that now. Do you think it is right to expect him to give that away for ...'

'A girl like me?' Kate finished his question for him. Nothing had changed, she wouldn't trust him.

'That's not what I was going to say.'

'I have already told you …' Kate stopped talking as Amanda Collins poured coffee at the table.

'Tell me about you and Captain Brannigan?' Commodore Hale said.

Kate noticed that the Commodore had used the rank 'Captain' in his reference to Michael; she could not hide her feelings. She wanted to keep this conversation appropriate, not show him how she felt.

'Michael has filled an empty space in my soul,' she said. 'I love him more than I thought was possible.'

Then she said, 'Michael has waited too long for this.' She hadn't really known how long until now. He had kept that from her.

'Captain Brannigan has made it very clear to me that he will marry you at any cost,' Commodore Hale said.

'I know that,' she said.

She sipped her coffee – it gave her space to think. She didn't want to be here; it was getting too hard to hide. She took a slow breath.

'I have already told you I will not stand in the way of his promotion,' she said.

'Tell me about your husband,' he said.

'My husband is dead. How many times do I have to tell you?' She hadn't meant to say that aloud.

'I know. I am sorry. Please tell me.'

'Why are Patrick's beliefs so important? They weren't mine.'

'You have already met Steven Jacobs. He is not the only one to harbour such animosity. You must be aware nothing will stop their paranoia. Many people have helped us, who we will turn on.'

How could she forget that man, his cold eyes, his hatred? Kate had no doubt Michael would protect her and the girls, but could he protect himself?

'How can you be so sure?'

'I can.'

She couldn't let Patrick down. They had looked after each other for most of their lives. Now they would both fight for Michael.

She said, 'We weren't much more than children when the depression started. Patrick was able to get some work at the biscuit factory. He was cheap labour, but at least it was some money for his mum. He made friends with some older men who took him to meetings, trying to get better wages and conditions for the workers. It was hard for Patrick, not having enough to eat, not being paid a proper wage. We were lucky we had our dad.'

He reached across the table and placed his hand over hers. Was this appropriate? Should she remove her hand? Was he trying to be kind?

It was such a different world he came from. The same world Michael came from. Michael, who was prepared to give that world away because he loved her.

She couldn't let that happen.

'Patrick wasn't really old enough to join the Communist Party, but he attended meetings and rallies. He thought it would help; he thought people would be better off. He wasn't the only one. The party wasn't very well thought of, better than the fascist but not much. He wasn't involved by the time we got married.'

There was nothing else she wanted to say, and while he was being kind and treating her with respect, she just wanted to go home.

He said, 'Kate, when the war ends, we are going to need men like Captain Brannigan. We can't have him doing anything rash.'

She wanted to ask him when that would be. When would the war end? When would Michael come home to her?

'Michael must keep his Command. I will not let him give that away,' Kate said.

'Do you think you can stop him?' he asked.

'I can try.'

She could try – she would have to survive on her own – she could try.

Then he asked, 'Does Captain Brannigan know?'

He had noticed!

She shook her head, no.

'He has a right to know,' Commodore Hale said.

'And I have a right to tell him,' Kate said. She pushed her fingertips up to her eyes: she didn't want to do that.

They were interrupted by the arrival of a young man in a naval uniform. He saluted and addressed the Commodore.

'I'm sorry, Kate. I have to go,' he said. 'Can I give you a lift home?'

'No, thank you. I would like to walk.'

He rose from the table. Kate stayed seated.

Chapter Twenty-seven

Kate and Frank walked arm in arm along a sandy beach, under clear autumn skies. It was Tuesday, May 8th, 1945.

'Shall we rest?' she asked.

He had been discharged from the hospital. His wounds were healing, but he walked with a stick, and his eyesight was severely damaged.

'Yes,' Frank Kelly said.

Kate knew how tired he was, and she knew he'd been fighting with his mother over her and Michael.

'Let's find a seat.' Kate guided him to a bench on the grass. They'd had very little time together since his return and, as she sat next to him, he asked her, 'Are you all right, Kate?'

'Yes, I'm fine.'

'Kate?'

'Nothing's wrong, Frank. I'm pregnant … I'm going to have Michael's baby.'

He took her hands. 'You are happy?'

'Oh, yes, Frank. I'm happy.'

'What's all this then?' He wiped the tears from her cheeks.

'I've been stupid. Michael doesn't know. I didn't tell him. After that man Jacobs, I was afraid. I thought I could make him give me up, maybe I still can, but if he knows about the baby he never would.'

'Do you really think he would give you up, Kate?'

She shrugged and reached for the gold locket around her neck. 'I've been stupid. I should have told him – he does have a right to know.'

'Not stupid, my dear, just frightened. He will be happy, and he will do what he needs to do, and so will you.'

'Be my friend about the baby, won't you – don't be the priest. Maybe it doesn't quite fit the rules.' She was breaking all the rules they grew up with.

'I'll be your friend,' Frank Kelly said. His face showed the questions he was trying to answer for himself.

Kate took his hand.

'When is the baby due?' he asked as a friend should.

'November.'

'Will everything be all right? What does Joshua say?'

'Yes, everything will be all right,' Kate replied.

Kate turned the corner into Solomon Street. She saw the boy on the bicycle; stood motionless as he passed. *Make yourself invisible, he might not see you.* The boy nodded his head as he rode past her. When her legs felt strong enough, she continued walking up the hilly street.

'Kate!' Peg called.

Kate reached for the support of her front gate and turned to her friend.

'Kate, Billy's alive!' Peg waved the telegram in her hand, 'He's alive!'

Two women fell into each other's arms.

'Alive, Kate. The telegram says 'wounded but recovering and will be coming home soon'.'

Tears fell. Tears of happiness could hide other fears.

Suddenly the street was full of voices: women gathered in the open; church bells rang in the distance. Kate and Peg joined the gathering crowd.

'The war is over!'

Women danced arm in arm, sharing the joy.

Michael will be safe.

'Germany has surrendered,' a voice said.

'Germany?'

'Germany?' Kate heard her own voice, 'What about us?'

'On the wireless, the announcement said that soon we can expect Japan to surrender.' Another voice.

You are not safe yet.

Kate returned to her front gate.

'Kate …' Peg put her arm around Kate's shoulder. '… it won't be long now. Everyone says so.' Then she said, 'We are going to Helen's to celebrate. Come with us.'

Peg was happy, Billy was safe; the war really was over for her. Soon her husband would be home after so many years away, and she wanted to celebrate.

Kate was happy Billy was safe. She had known him most of her life, and she was happy for Peg. But she remembered the hurtful words Peg had said. Sometimes they rang so loudly in her ears. 'Whore', Peg had called her. She'd been drunk, but it still hurt. Then Tilly had wanted to know what that dreadful word meant. The Ferguson boy was using it on the way home from school. She had come to understand he was talking about her. She had only ever been with two men: one her neighbours and friends had known for many years, and one they hadn't even bothered to get to know.

Peg wanted to celebrate. Kate could see she wanted to share her happiness with her, maybe that was not possible anymore. 'You go Peg,' Kate said. 'I'll see you later.'

Chapter Twenty-eight

It was strange to celebrate the ending of a war while men were still dying, but that is what happened – all the next day and into the evening. Peg asked Kate to join her and some friends from the street for a party in the evening. Kate agreed, for Peg's sake, and it was arranged for the girls to sleep at their grandparents.

The Orion Hotel was a better known and more respectable establishment. Kate and Peg joined their neighbours in the lounge. The old building had been used as a public house for more than a century. It had high ceilings, large rooms and polished floors. Tonight, tables and chairs surrounded a crowded, smoke-filled dance floor. Couples danced, and a band played music.

Kate watched Peg dance with Ray Ferguson while she made stilted conversation with his wife, Helen.

'Your turn, Katey,' Ray said as he returned Peg to the table. 'Can't have you sitting all alone while you look so pretty, can we?'

She knew how she looked. Michael's dress was a perfect fit, for now, and the style and colours suited her. Ray held her too tight when they danced. After another dance, she insisted he returned her to the table, saying that Helen might like a dance. The hatred in Helen Ferguson's eyes frightened Kate. She excused herself from the table and pushed her way through the crowds to the ladies room. She stayed there as long as she could before returning to the table.

The table was empty. Ray was dancing with his wife, and Peg had found someone to dance with. She sat alone, enjoying the music, remembering the time she had danced with Michael, the first and the only time. There hadn't been any other opportunities for dancing – maybe one day, when the war was over.

'Excuse me, ma'am, would you care to dance?'

The accent was right, but the voice was young, and she turned to refuse him. He had dark eyes, and a shy smile hovered around his mouth. His skin was pale, almost white, and his dark brown curls were cropped short. He was tall, and he stood awkwardly, waiting for her answer.

'Thank you.'

He lost his shyness as they danced. He talked about his shipmates, his sweetheart and his parents back home. She enjoyed his company during the dances they shared and then he returned her to the table.

Two friends ran up Solomon Street, girls on a night out – they both knew that tonight would be the last night they would share like this. The cold wind blowing in over the ocean bought icy raindrops that chased the girls up the road. They ran onto the veranda of Peg's home, opened the front door, pulled the curtains shut, turned the lights on and flopped onto her bed.

'It was a good night, wasn't it?' Peg said.

'It was.'

'It won't be the same now, will it?'

'No,' Kate said.

'It's been a long war.'

It still going on. Kate thought. 'Too long,' she said.

Rain fell heavily as Kate ran across the road and onto her veranda. The dark night swallowed her, and she rushed to put her key in the lock.

'Wish you were here, Sam,' she said.

She missed him. The security he gave her with his presence at her door, but mostly she missed his companionship.

She shook water from her coat as she entered the dark house and pushed the front door shut. Kate turned the light on. The door did not shut properly, and she hurried to close it, but it opened.

'What are you doing here?' Kate asked.

'Just come to see that you got home safely,' Ray Ferguson said.

He was holding her door open, leaning on it.

'As you can see, I did.'

He pushed the door shut and came into her home.

'Helen will be wondering where you are.' The words sounded more potent than she felt.

'Na, she won't.'

Kate backed down the hallway. 'What do you want?'

He moved quickly, grabbing her arms tightly.

'Let me go.'

'What's wrong, Katey? I know about you. I saw you dancing with that Yankee sailor tonight. You've been at it a long time. I saw you on the beach before Christmas; I saw you here on our street the other day with another bloody Yankee sailor. I know all about you.'

'Let me go.'

Her words were barely audible above the rain on the roof. His grip was firm; she pushed him away with a strength she didn't know she possessed, but he was much stronger than her.

He forced her against the wall, grabbed her face in his hand and turned her mouth to his. He smelt of liquor and stale tobacco. She couldn't breathe. With all her strength, she ran her fingernails down his cheek. He yelled out in pain and let her body free; she slumped to the floor. Kate pushed herself to her feet; stumbled to the front door and opened it, but he was right behind her and slammed it shut.

'You fucking bitch!' He threw her down the hall. She slammed into a solid jarrah door frame, and her body crumpled to the floor. She tried to move, but nothing happened. *Move!* She couldn't. Warm liquid trickled through her hair; pain erupted in her shoulder. She tried again to move, but her legs wouldn't support her, so she backed away from him on her haunches.

Tight rough hands gripped her arms and forced her body to the floor. He knelt over her and tore open her dress, ripping her skin with his fingernails. Blood trickled over the gold locket that lay between her breasts. He took the locket in his hand.

'No!' She covered his hand. 'Please.'

'What you making all this fuss about? I've heard about you. Whore! I'm as good as any fucking Yankee sailor. Why are you making such a fuss?' He touched his blood-streaked cheek. 'You shouldn't have hurt me.'

He wrenched the locket from her, flung it down the hallway.

'No!' she screamed.

He struggled with his trousers, forced her to the floor, held her down with his knees. She had to protect her baby, and looked him in the eyes and asked, 'Why, Ray?'

***

Michael Brannigan stood on the bridge of the Codfish. He removed the looking-glasses he scanned the ocean with. A warm wind blew across the vessel as it made its way through a calm sea on a still night. He shuddered as a chill ran through his body.

'You okay, Captain?' Seaman Emerson asked.

'Yes.'

His heart raced.

'No,' he whispered. 'You promised.'

'Sir?'

'Nothing.'

He stood straight and shook his head.

'Let's go down and check those maps,' he said.

Chapter Twenty-nine

Kate opened her eyes. She could hear a voice, a woman saying 'What have you done? What have you done?' She was cold and couldn't move. A warm coat covered her. Footsteps padded down the hallway to the front door. A male voice said, 'Kate needs our help, Peg. Can you get the doctor?'

There was no answer, and the voice said again, 'Peg, can you get the doctor?'

'Yes, yes,' Kate heard the reply.

'Michael.' She could see an outline in the doorway and tried to sit. Movement brought pain. She closed her eyes. Hands touched her – not Michael's. She tried to push them away.

'Kate?'

That voice – not Michael.

'Don't hurt me,' she pleaded. 'Don't hurt me.'

'I won't hurt you, Kate. Look at me … open your eyes.'

'Joe?' She opened her eyes and could see him kneeling on the floor beside her.

'Yes, Kate.'

She tried to move to seek contact with him, a safe place.

'I'm cold.'

'Can you move?' he asked.

'It hurts.' She struggled with the words.

'Where?' he asked.

'Michael,' Kate mumbled.

She closed her eyes. He was gentle when he picked her up, and she tried not to cry out as he moved her. He buttoned his coat around her before putting her in her bed and pulling the blankets across her. She began to shiver, mumbling. 'I'm sorry. I couldn't let him hurt our baby. I'm sorry.'

The jacket was warm and made of the same material Michael wore – it had the same oily smell. She breathed deeply.

The voice said, 'I'm here, Kate. Everything is okay, I'm here.' It wasn't Michael. But she trusted that voice and let him hold her; she needed the warmth his body offered.

Another voice said, 'I would like to see her alone.'

'Michael,' Kate cried as Joe left the bed.

'The doctor's here. He will look after you now,' Joe said.

Her blanket was pulled back, and the buttons on the khaki coat that kept her warm were undone. Gentle hands use a warm cloth to bath her injuries.

In the kitchen, Joseph Daniels sat at the table while Peg Kennedy prepared tea, filling the pot and placing it in front of him. When Kate cried out, Peg began to weep.

When Joshua Fredericks entered the room, Joseph Daniels stood. The two men introduced themselves, and Joe asked. 'How is she?'

'I have cleaned and dressed her wounds, and I have given her something to help her sleep. She has suffered shock, and lying on the floor all night didn't do her any good.'

'The child?' Joe said. 'Is the child unharmed?'

Peg stifled her cry.

'Are you the father?'

'No.'

Joshua Fredericks said. 'As far as I can tell, the baby is unharmed. Kate has been hurt, but she was not raped. The baby should be safe in the womb.'

'Can I see her?' Joe asked. 'I'm leaving for home in a few hours.'

'Only for a short while,' he said. 'I will see her parents on my way back, and she has asked to see Frank.'

'I will let him know,' Joe said. 'I'm calling on him on my way back to the dock.'

In the bedroom, the nurse went about her duties.

'Her pretty dress is all ruined,' she told Joe as he entered the room.

'Dresses can be replaced,' he said. Then he asked, 'Is she comfortable?'

'She's sleeping … best not to wake her.'

The nurse folded the torn and stained dress and placed it at the end of the bed.

'She had this clenched in her hand,' she said and handed Joe a blood-stained gold locket.

***

Kate stirred. She could see a man in a uniform. *Not Michael.* 'Joe?' she said.

Joe sat on the bed and took her hand. 'Tell Michael I … I'm sorry … I should have told him about … you were right … love him.'

'He knows you love him, Kate, and he will be happy about the baby. I will see you very soon when you come home with him.'

He placed the locket in her hand.

'This is yours,' he said. He kissed her forehead and said, 'Goodbye, Kate.'

She folded her hands into her chest, holding the precious object close and let sleep overtake her.

When Kate next opened her eyes, Frank was sitting on the chair beside her bed. She could see the anger and sorrow on his face. She reached her hand out to him. He pushed her hair away from her face.

'Frank?'

'I'm here.' He took her hand and held it gently.

'I had to protect the baby. I tried to fight him, but I couldn't. Joshua said the baby should be all right. I tried to fight him …' She couldn't put her words together.

'Who did this to you, Kate? You should tell the police,' Frank said.

157

'No, Frank, no! People will say it was my fault.'

'Do you want to tell me?'

'Only as my friend.' He would understand she wanted him, the boy next door, the boy she had grown up with, who she loved, who loved her, who she had shared so much with.

He sat on the bed and took her in his arms. 'Tell me then?'

'Only you … only you.'

She told him. Still fighting the sleeping potion, she said, 'Frank, how can people … dreadful things. I love Michael. What harm did we do? We never hurt anyone. Why?'

'I'm sorry, Kate,' he said.

She cried. And he held her until she slept.

Chapter Thirty

Kate would take time to recover. She would never understand the reason she was a victim of such an attack; it was too hard to understand. She explained away her bruises and injuries to the girls, saying she had slipped on the back step and fallen. She would not speak to her neighbours again, except for Peg and even that friendship would not be quite the same. Kate forbade Tilly from visiting a house at the bottom of the street, saying that May was welcome to come to their home, but Tilly was not allowed to go there. Tilly seemed to understand not to argue about this.

In that house at the bottom of the street, a wife listened to her husband explain away the scratches on his face and had to believe him.

At the end of May, Kate and her mother took the girls to York, a small farming community northeast of the city. Kathleen O'Brien's brother owned this property. It was a trip Kate had made for most years of her life, a family holiday. Now, with the farm short-handed, they were able to help with the harvesting of the snow pea crop.

Kate had excused herself from the fieldwork and was on home duties, cooking and cleaning. She sat on the back veranda in the winter sun and looked down the green rolling hills that seemed to go on to the horizon.

'Kate,' her mother called as she came out the back door.

'I'm here,' Kate replied.

Kathleen sat on the empty chair beside her.

'I have something to tell you, Mum,' Kate said. 'You know I'm pregnant?'

'I thought you might be.'

'Please don't be angry. I told Michael I couldn't have any more children. He said it didn't matter but …'

'I'm not angry.'

'He doesn't even know yet, Mum. I wish he knew, I wish we could share this,' Kate said.

'Don't you remember what Dr Fredericks said after you had Jessie?' her mother asked.

'Yes,' Kate remembered. *Such a lot of fuss.*

'Does Michael know this?'

'No, and he must not. Don't worry, everything will be okay.'

'What about the girls?'

It was such happy news, she wanted to be able to share it.

'I'm sure Jessie will be happy. Tilly may need more time.'

'Your father?' Kathleen asked.

'Soon, Mum, I'll tell him soon. It is wonderful news, Mum. I want everyone to be happy. I wish I'd told Michael.'

The sun was low in the sky and the shadows were growing long.

'Time to get food ready for the hungry workers.' Kate rose from the chair and exclaimed, 'Mum!'

'What?' her mother asked anxiously.

Kate placed her hand on her stomach. 'My baby's alive, Mum! He's alive; he's moving.'

She took her mother's hand and placed it on the spot where she had felt the movement. It was too early for her mother to feel, but for Kate, it was the movement that told her her baby was alive and unharmed. She had waited for this, it seemed so long, even though she knew it wasn't.

'Yes,' Kathleen O'Brien said. Her gentle face beaming, she said to her daughter, 'He?'

Kate told the girls she was going to have a baby. Jessie seemed to understand and asked if 'Tenant Michael knew about his baby. Kate told her they would tell him when he came home. Then we will be a family, Jessie told her. She hugged Kate and asked if she was getting a sister or brother. Kate said she would have to wait and see if she was getting a brother or sister. The love and excitement Jessie showed for her unborn sibling filled Kate with hope and happiness.

Tilly reacted as Kate expected, upset and annoyed. Kate had told her how babies were made. And Kate had told her you were supposed to wait until you were married and now look at what she had done. How could she do this to her? What was everyone going to say at school? Kate said she was sorry, but she and Michael would be married soon, maybe it wouldn't seem so bad then. After that there was nothing more to say.

Kate walked down the laneway to her parents' home. It was a cold day in early June. It was time to talk to her father.

Looking up from the paper he was reading, Sean O'Brien glanced at his wife who was at the stove stirring a pot.

'You have something to tell me, Kate?'

'Yes, Dad.'

Kate stood beside the table. Looking down on her father should have given her an advantage. She turned to her mother and took the hand offered.

'Sean,' Kathleen O'Brien cautioned.

'It's okay, Mum. I'm sorry, Dad. I love Michael, and I am going to have his baby.'

Kate began to feel a slight advantage. 'You must have guessed.'

'Yes. Your mother has already told me if I had any doubts.'

He pushed his chair hard behind him as he stood. Kate was once again that little girl who had done something she shouldn't. Beloved by her father, but in trouble all the same.

'For God's sake, Kate, why did you let this happen? You should have been more careful.'

'Sean,' his wife said.

'Why didn't you think. What did Michael think you were doing?'

Kate stared dumbly at her father. She had not expected him to be so angry; he was a kind and gentle man, and she had rarely seen him in a rage.

'We'll be married soon,' was all she could say.

'Ah,' he fumed and turned away from her.

Kate knew he was overreacting. She knew he had found out who hurt her. He tried to make her report this to the police. She had refused and asked him not to do anything silly, not to take the matter into his own hands. He was angry but did as she asked.

'Come on, Sean,' came the gentle, soothing voice of her mother. That voice had always kept him calm in any family crisis. 'They are to be married soon.'

'Yes,' he calmed himself.

He turned to Kate and said, 'I've seen submarines leave the harbour – some never return. All those strong, healthy men, just gone, swallowed by the sea. What if this happens …'

Kate couldn't see. She began to tremble. Her legs wouldn't hold her, and she gripped the back of the chair before slipping to the floor.

'Kate,' she heard her mother cry.

Her father reached her as she hit the floor.

'He'll be all right, Kate. He'll be all right,' he said.

Her father sat on the floor, holding her. She could not cry.

She stared into his eyes. What was he saying?

'He'll be all right. Michael will be all right,' she heard the words.

Chapter Thirty-one

Kate was restless. It was the second week in June, and the Codfish should be back in port. She'd been gone for nearly seven weeks. She sat in front of the kitchen stove, keeping warm as she mixed cake in a bowl on her knee. The knock on the door startled her.

Michael! He would knock.

She threw the bowl on the table, pulled her jumper over her stomach and looked in the mirror on the hallway wall. She was pregnant: he would be able to tell. He would hold her in his gentle, loving arms. They would talk; she would tell him everything. He would make love with her. His hands would be kind and tender. He would wash away the uncertainty – she would be in the arms of the man who loved her.

He stood before her, a boy unknown, an envelope in his hand.

'Mrs Kelly?' he asked.

'Yes.'

She took the envelope and watched him walk away.

Her fingers fought with the paper in the dimly lit hallway as she tried to make out the words. She stumbled into the brighter kitchen and fell onto the table.

'Sit down, Kate.' Peg took Kate's arm and sat her on the chair. She moved the kettle to the middle of the stove, opened the front of the fire and put tea in the pot before taking the telegram from Kate.

'It's all right, Kate,' she said.

Peg poured water onto the tea leaves and put the pot on the table.

'I can't live like this,' Kate whispered.

'Yes, you can,' Peg said as she sat opposite Kate.

Kate shook her head.

'You have Jessie and Michael's baby, now drink your tea.'

The hot liquid warmed Kate and the coldness began to fade. Warmth returned to her body.

Peg said, 'Now read the telegram again. Read it slowly.'

Kate read. *Safe and well. Michael.*

'Michael's safe and well, he said so,' Peg said. 'And you are going to be married and everything is going to be just fine.'

Kate moved her chair closer to the fire. Patrick had left the old wood-burning stove in the kitchen when he had put in the new gas one. It kept her warm on many cold winter days. She read the telegram again. She understood Michael would not have wanted to send it. And she understood he would not be coming back soon and that he did not want her to be waiting in fear.

'Better now?' Peg asked.

Kate nodded her head yes. The words on the piece of paper she clutched tightly made that possible. Her child moved, reminding her he was alive; she was alive; she was right to protect him. She folded her arms across her stomach.

'Yes,' she said, 'It's going to be okay.'

***

Michael Brannigan sat on a sandy beach and looked out over a blue ocean. Hot sunshine reflected off white sand and a gentle breeze pushed small waves onto the shore.

It was an interesting and varied patrol, his first in command. The Codfish had travelled further north than before, picking up downed aircrew and returning them to ships. His crew had shown him courage and loyalty. They were disappointed, as he was, when they were told they would not be returning to Fremantle. They were to refuel and take on supplies at the base on the North West coast of Australia. Beer rations were arranged, and time off given. It was a desolate place they were in and, like him, they would be happy to be back at sea.

He had written to his mother and daughter, and now he wrote to Kate. He saw her watching his departure, rain wetting her face as she smiled bravely at him. She had become so crucial to his happiness, sometimes he felt quite stunned by this. The uneasy feeling he had for her safety early in May had faded. Sending Kate the cable was difficult, but she would be waiting, and a letter could take weeks to arrive. He could not let her worry like that, and he knew she would understand. He looked at the words he had written. What could he say? She knew he loved her, but he told her anyway; he told her he hoped they would marry when he returned to port. There was much to say but the mail had to be censored before posting. He had to do this for his crew, and he would write no more than they were allowed. He finished his letter in the simplest words. 'Remember I will love you forever.'

He folded the paper and sealed it in an envelope.

'Excuse me, sir.'

'Yes, Emerson,' Michael answered the young seaman.

'Sir, the 'Chief' said could you come back to the boat?'

'I'll be right there.'

He dismissed Emerson, who turned and walked along the beach to the pier and the boat. He addressed the letter and put it in his left pocket to be posted separately from the ones in his other pocket.

Chapter Thirty-two

Kate and her family, along with thirty thousand other people, attended the funeral of the Australian Prime Minister John Curtin on 8th July 1945. For many, this man was the greatest hero in their country's history. He had defied Winston Churchill and withdrew Australian troops from Africa, bringing them home to defend their own country. When the British Empire was unable to help them, he turned to America for an alliance. What would have happened to them if he hadn't done that? – the Japanese had bombed Darwin and Broome, that wasn't so far away.

Kate received Michael's letter that week and knew she would not see him again until the war was over. She visited the doctor and did what she was told, most of the time.

Prison camps were liberated and, as the Japanese drew back towards their homeland, the cruelty and horror of war were exposed again.

Tilly continued to write to her father. The news out of the prison camps was agonising, and Kate struggled to keep Tilly calm.

Kate's pregnancy became obvious to her neighbours. Some still gossiped – one woman in a house at the bottom of the street did not join in this gossip.

Peg Kennedy prepared for husband's return. She received a letter from the doctors but nothing from Billy himself. He arrived back in Fremantle towards the end of July and Peg rushed to the hospital to be with him.

***

Kate stood at the back door. 'No, Peg,' she said.

Peg sat at her kitchen table, a glass in her hand and a bottle in the other. 'He didn't even know who I was,' she said, tears running down her face. 'I was so happy. I should have paid more attention to the doctor's letter.

'He just stared blankly at me – he didn't even know my name,' Peg said. 'It was awful. Men screaming and crying, but worse just sitting and staring, staring not knowing who they were. The doctor said they found him in the jungle – he wasn't hurt, he didn't know who he was or why he was in the jungle. Maybe he's deliberately trying to forget.'

'Oh, Peg.'

'What am I going to do?'

'You will help him remember … and you don't need this.' Kate took the bottle and poured the contents down the sink.

Kate and Peg sat on the back veranda, Kate pouring tea. Peg had been visiting Billy every day. She told Kate Billy had called her name when she arrived at the hospital this morning. She hoped it meant he remembered. But he seemed to only remember who she was and what she told him on her previous visits.

'I don't know what to do,' Peg said. 'The doctors suggested bringing him home. Seeing people and places he knows might help. But what about Harry? He won't understand. He doesn't really know who he is. What will I tell him?'

Kate was in her front garden. Peg and Billy Kennedy walked up the hilly street. Peg held his arm, and neighbours stopped to talk, but he became agitated and hostile. Kate left her lifeless rose bush and went to meet them.

'Billy,' Peg said, 'this is Kate. You remember Patrick and Kate.'

Blank, empty eyes stared at Kate.

'Hello, Billy,' Kate said.

Billy Kennedy placed his hand on Kate's pregnant belly. He looked at her face and then at his hand. 'Patrick died,' he said.

'Yes.'

The veil across his eyes moved. 'It was a long time ago.'

'Yes,' Kate whispered.

Billy Kennedy said, 'Patrick said to tell you he loved you and he was sorry. He said you knew he wouldn't be coming home.'

There was nothing to say.

Billy turned to his wife and said, 'Don't cry, Peggy. Let's go home.'

Billy Kennedy began the slow and painful restoration of his life. He would never again be the same free spirit he was, but he would be a devoted husband and good father to his only child.

Chapter Thirty-three

Kate walked along the ocean shore. The last day of July was cold, the still water reflected the sunshine, but there was no warmth in the air. She wore Michael's jumper; his scent lingered on the fabric. She buried herself in that scent. She wanted his tender hands on her, his gentle touch, his arms around her. She wanted to listen to his heartbeat after they shared their bodies. Their child stirred, and she wrapped her arms around her stomach. She should have told him. She wanted him to feel his child alive in her belly.

Kate found a bench on the grass; took Michael's letter from her trouser pocket and reread it. She closed her eyes and saw the grin that wrinkled up his face, his brown eyes, warm and gentle; she heard his laughter.

'*Kate,*' he called.

She was alone, a solitary seagull's squawk her only comfort. Kate read the letter again.

A gust of wind, the first of the day, startled her and she looked out across the ocean. Dark grey clouds sat on the horizon, and she shuddered, folded the letter and hurried home.

The house was safe and warm; the threatening storm sat off the coast, and there was an uneasy calm in the early night. Kate and the girls sat in the front room. The burning fire kept them warm as they occupied themselves.

'Mummy?' Jessie asked.

Kate looked up from her book.

'Mummy is 'Tenant Michael coming back?'

'Yes, of course.'

'Mummy, some of the big girls at school said that submarines never come back, because they get sunk and nobody can escape, and they all get drowned.'

Kate took Jessie in her arms.

'Michael's coming back to us. He's been away before and has come back, hasn't he?'

Kate tried to hide her eyes. She hadn't meant to hold Jessie so tight.

Jessie said, 'I was scared, Mummy, when they said that.'

'Don't worry, darling, he'll be all right. We have to tell him about our baby, don't we? He couldn't come home to us, you know that, but he wrote us a letter, didn't he?'

'Yes,' Jessie nodded.

'Time for bed,' Kate said.

'I'll take Jessie to bed,' Tilly offered.

She took the child's hand and helped her from Kate's knee.

'Thank you.'

Kate sat motionless in her chair. She hoped she had masked her feelings, not wanting to let her fears overtake her. She did not want her child to be overwhelmed by them. Kate pushed the dangers Michael faced away and thought of him in command and control. Jessie's words had brought the fears back, but she would drive them away again.

Kate rose from the chair, but her legs would not support her. Darkness surrounded her and forced her back to the chair. She could not move. Bracing her hands on the arms of the chair, she made herself stand. She did not recognise the woman looking back at her from the mirror over the fireplace.

'Mummy?'

A child was calling. Her child was calling.

'I'm coming.'

Kate woke screaming. Sweat covered her body. Rain pelted on the rooftop and, in the lightning, she saw the silhouette of a young woman in the doorway.

'What's wrong, Kate? Are you all right?' Tilly asked.

Tilly turned on the bedroom light. The raging storm shook the house; she came into the bedroom and stood by the bed.

'Kate!' She shook her arm. 'Kate!'

Kate turned to look at Tilly.

Tilly shook her harder. 'Kate!'

Kate blinked her eyes. 'Tilly?'

'What's wrong?'

Kate shook her head. 'Nothing. I'm all right. It was just a bad dream. Go back to bed.'

'No, I think I should get nana.'

***

Matilda O'Brien was frightened. Kate was white, and her skin was wet. What if something was wrong with the baby? She was angry, and they had argued; she had said terrible things about the baby to Kate. What if something was wrong?

'It's okay, Tilly.' Kate took her hand and she sat in the bed. 'It's not the baby, I'm all right ... it was just a bad dream.'

'I don't really want anything bad to happen.'

'I know that.'

***

Kate shuddered. Nature shook the little house as the sky lit up. The pain that woke her was fading – it was nothing to do with the baby, she knew that.

'Mummy, Mummy!' Jessie screamed.

'I'm coming.'

'I'll get her,' Tilly said.

Jessie ran to her, hiding under the covers as the storm raged outside. Tilly stood in the doorway.

'Come to bed, Tilly, it's cold out there,' Kate said.

Tilly turned out the light and climb into bed, and Kate pulled the blankets around them. They huddled together as the storm threw rain on the windows, as it broke branches from trees and lifted iron from roofs before it moved inland. The last winds of the storm played with the house, while Jessie and Tilly slept peacefully.

Kate stared at the ceiling. It had to be a dream, so clear and so real. The ocean was on fire; dark clouds illuminated by the glow. A plane flew soundlessly towards her. *Pain, so much pain.* Voices screamed and cried out. A blood-covered hand reached for her. She fought for him, but he slipped, slipped and disappeared under the oily water.

Chapter Thirty-four

North Pacific Ocean, August 1945

The United States Submarine Codfish wallowed in the swell. She wasn't built for surface work and was struggling with the wind and waves. Her crew was picking up airmen from a B 29 Bomber that had run out of fuel and ditched in the ocean – it was one of the many duties they performed. Storm clouds covered the last of the night-time stars. The lookouts were straining their eyes in the dark that comes before the dawn. Machine gun bullets hitting the deck was the first indication something was wrong.

***

Michael Brannigan saw the plane as it headed towards them. It was silent, no engines running. Was it out of fuel or it had deliberately turned off its engines? It was too late to sound the alarm. His machine gunners were in position, but could not get a lock on the target.

The plane hit them.

Fire exploded.

Men screamed.

The ocean was on fire; his boat was on fire. He knew she wasn't going to survive. He had to give the order to abandon her.

He stood in the Conning Tower, his back to the metal turret as he gave his orders. His crew moved swiftly and quietly, helping each other, the wounded put in the lifeboats first.

'Sir, the lifeboats are away,' Jack Morgan said.

Michael knew he had to move to get into the last lifeboat, but his boat was dying. Could he leave her?

'Sir!' Jack Morgan repeated.

Rain began to fall. Oil on the water would still burn, but maybe it would help with the fire on board. His executive officer stood beside him.

'Captain,' Lieutenant McDougal said, his hand pointing to the horizon. The cruiser came into sight, silhouetted by the sunlight that sat on the horizon.

It was an enemy ship. The crew in the lifeboats would not have enough time to escape. The Codfish still had some life in her, her engines still running.

'Go below,' Michael ordered his men. 'See if you can get the torpedoes to fire.'

He moved, urging the Codfish forward, away from his men in the lifeboats, towards the oncoming vessel.

He was impatient as he waited for the 'Chief' and his second in command to complete their task. He scanned the ocean in front of his vessel to see if they were able to follow his orders, the Codfish moving towards the cruiser.

'Sir, the torpedoes won't fire – they're jammed. Water is coming in and the electrics are getting wet,' Jack Morgan said as he came up from below.

Michael took a deep breath and turned to his men. 'Abandon ship, 'Chief'.'

'Sir.'

'Abandon ship, 'Chief'.'

There was only one way his crew could survive – it was up to him.

'Follow my orders, 'Chief'.'

His men came to attention and saluted him; he pulled himself up straight and returned their salute. They turned and he watched them follow his orders, then he turn his attention back to his boat.

'Come on, old girl, we've got to save our crew,' he said.

Michael jammed the throttle forward, the submarine lurched and shuddered. He saw the tell-tale sign of a torpedoes' wake as it sped away from him.

'Good girl,' he said. 'Good girl.'

It was only one torpedo that had fired; he saw it strike the oncoming vessel. If he was lucky it would be enough.

His legs would not hold him anymore and he slid down the cold, blood-covered wall he'd been using as support, the deck of his boat covered in his blood.

Now he had time.

'I'm sorry, my darling,' he said. 'Look after our girls for me.

'Forgive me.'

Chapter Thirty-five

Fremantle, Western Australia,
August 1945

Kate was alone when she woke. She could hear the girls clattering around in the kitchen – they would be late for school. She had overslept.

She pushed her tangled hair behind her ears as she entered the kitchen.

'Good morning,' Kathleen O'Brien said.

'Where are the girls? What time is it?'

'The girls are at home with dad. It's nearly nine. Are you all right?' Kathleen said.

'Michael, I will,' Kate whispered.

She stumbled.

'Kate?' Her mother took her arms.

'I'm all right, Mum,' Kate said.

'Kate,' her mother scolded, 'the girls haven't even gone to school today. Tilly was crying this morning, saying you were screaming and seemed to be in pain last night. We kept them both at home. What's wrong? Are you in pain?'

Pain so much pain, but not hers.

'Not me, Mum,' Kate mumbled. 'Michael's dying.'

***

Kathleen O'Brien sat her daughter at the table and placed a teacup and toast before her.

'Nonsense, Kate, it is not possible for you to know that,' she said. 'Eat your food and when you're finished, we are going to see the doctor.'

'I'm not hungry.'

Kathleen sat opposite her daughter.

'Eat, Kate. You have to look after yourself. Michael's baby needs you to do that.'

She had never interfered in Kate's life, always knowing that she would be sensible and would do what she had too.

'Eat your food. The children need you to be well. If anything happens to Michael, I'm sure you will be informed. Even then you must continue on with your life, he is relying on you to do that.'

'I can't, Mum.'

Kathleen spoke the hardest words now. Ones she never wanted to use. 'You will have too.'

'I...' Kate turned her face away from her mother.

Kathleen stood and walked around the table; she took her daughter's face in her hands and looked into her eyes.

'It is your duty, Kate. Just as Michael has his duty, so do you, to his children, to Jessie and to your brother's child.'

'I don't ...'

'There is no choice Kate. Understand? No choice! We need you here.'

***

Kate saw in her mother's eyes the desperate fear she had kept hidden all these years. The fear for her only son.

'Oh, Mum,' Kate shuddered. 'How can we do this?'

'Hush now,' her mother said. 'Hush.'

Kathleen poured tea from the pot with a hand that was almost still. 'Drink your tea.'

Kate dressed and joined her mother in front of Joshua Fredericks' desk.

'Everything is as it should be,' he said. 'Now I want you to see a specialist.'

'Why?' Kate asked. 'I don't want to see any other doctor ... you delivered Jessie.'

'Kate, you haven't listened to anything I've told you.'

He glanced at her mother. 'When you first came to see me …'

'Yes, I know,' Kate cut him off mid-sentence. She didn't want to hear all that again. 'I feel fine; the baby's alive and growing.'

'Kate, the problem's not the carrying, you know that it's the delivering.' He turned to her mother.

'Listen to the doctor, Kate, he is only trying to help, to make sure everything is all right,' Kathleen said.

Kate sat on the wicker chair on her back veranda. It was the ninth day of August. A cold winter's day blew around her, but she was unaware of it. She did not hear the back gate open so his fingers on her cheeks startled her.

'Sometimes it's so real,' she said.

'Yes,' Sean O'Brien said.

He sat on the chair beside her and took her hand, the pain she was feeling faded.

'What's wrong, Dad?' There was concern in her father's eyes. She was not the only one waiting on news. *Please not Robert, I can't tell Tilly.* 'Is it Robert?' she asked.

'No, we have no news on Robert,' her father said. 'Have you been listening to the wireless?'

'No.'

'Another Japanese city has been destroyed,' he said. 'The war must end now.'

'Was it just a single bomb?'

'Yes.'

'How can that be, Dad?' she asked.

Her father shrugged and said, 'They must surrender now.'

'Yes,' Kate said. 'They must.'

She folded her arms across her stomach. What kind of world was in store for her children? Jessie six, nearly seven and her child yet to be born. A world with the knowledge to make weapons that could destroy cities with a single bomb. Maybe they would be a deterrent; maybe they would put a stop to the never-ending war.

'Let's go and meet the girls. They'll be on their way home soon,' Kate said.

Her father helped her from her chair and, with his arm around her, they went to meet the children.

Chapter Thirty-six

The war did end, six days later, in the middle of August 1945. It was over. Once again, a beautiful blue and green sphere that orbits an ordinary star began the task of gathering its shattered pieces together.

The end of the war was celebrated. Peopled danced, sang and cried. Church bells rang out. Six years of fighting, of sending men away to die, ended. Children had been born. Girls had grown into women. Youths had become men. Women had become widows, children fatherless and men had lost women they loved.

***

Kate waited for word from Michael. Dreams kept her company, too real for dreams but what else could she call them, they had to be dreams. On a warm winter's day Kate returned home. She'd had another fruitless day searching for news of her brother. Her shopping bag was heavy, every step a mile long. Would there ever be any news of Robert? At least his name was not on the list of dead. She pushed the gate open – her garden was becoming crowded with weeds. She should get some planting done … it would all have to wait. The roses were life-less stems.

Michael.

'You have too,' she whispered.

Kate opened the front door and walked down the hallway into the kitchen. She saw the envelope on the kitchen table, put her bag on the floor and stepped towards the table.

***

Matilda O'Brien was waiting for word from her father. She had last seen him on a noisy, panic-filled dock as the ship she was on pulled away from Singapore harbour – she was eleven years old. She remembered him, but it was a long time since she's seen him. Would she recognise him? Would he recognise her? He was the only parent she remembered. Kate had become a friend and mother to her over the past three years.

She scanned newspapers, desperately searching photographs for faces that resemble his, reading names in stories in the hope his name might be mentioned. The war had been over for nearly two weeks.

'I'm scared, Kate,' she said.

Tears ran down her cheeks. She pushed the envelope towards Kate.

Kate pulled out a chair and sat. She picked up the envelope and pulled at the seal. It did not open easily, and her fingers tore the paper once it was out. Her eyes filling with tears, she handed the telegram to Kate.

'Daddy's alive! My daddy's alive!'

'Yes.'

Tilly hugged Kate and let the tears she had tried to hide all these years fall. Kate lifted her head and wiped her cheeks.

'I think Nana and Pop would like to know.'

'Yes.' Tilly kissed Kate. 'I'll go and tell them now.'

Tilly pushed the screen door so hard it swung back on its hinges before slamming shut as she ran down the back step.

On the twenty-fifth day of August 1945, Matilda O'Brien's war ended.

Chapter Thirty-seven

North Pacific Ocean. August 1945

Michael Brannigan could see sunlight through his closed eyelids. His face was warm, but his body hurt. Someone was kicking him. He didn't remember much about the last day. His boat was gone — had his crew made it to safety? He remembered the torpedo striking the oncoming cruiser, being pulled off the deck of the Codfish, supported in the water. That was about all. His men had disobeyed his orders by coming back for him.

He was being kicked again.

'Hey, cut that out,' he heard. It was the 'Chief'.

He opened his eyes. The sun was so bright he couldn't see. His pain was tempered by what he presumed was morphine from the boat's medical kit.

Someone looked in his face. He could not understand their words, but their actions were clear: he was to move. He tried. His body would not respond to his commands. Boots in his body again.

Chief Morgan helped him sit, and then Mr McDougal and the 'Chief' helped him to his feet. He could see they were on a sandy shore, the men with guns seemed so young, no more than school age. They were nervous. The Codfish had washed up on the reef: she was in pieces.

'The crew, 'Chief'?' he asked.

'Away safely in the dark, sir.'

The 'Chief' was struck with the butt of a rifle for his answer.

They were herded towards what looked like a makeshift campsite where their captors rummaged through their supplies and took them. They grabbed the water and shared it amongst themselves before allowing him and his men a share. He couldn't stand anymore, even with the help of his men, and he crumpled to the sand. He was shoved with a boot again. It wasn't going to make any difference; he couldn't move. He heard the Chief shouting, and he heard shouting in reply. He heard nothing.

It was dark when Michael opened his eyes again. *'No, Kate.'*

He was sure she was there. But he was alone.

A fire was burning, and his men and their captors were sitting around it.

'Chief.' He was helped to sit up and given some water.

'Sir, we have been able to get some extra supplies from the boat. I don't think these guys have had much to eat in the last week or so,' Chief Morgan told him.

'My orders, 'Chief'?'

'We did abandon ship, sir, but when the torpedo struck, and the other ship no longer threatened us we couldn't leave you behind, sir.'

Michael took the other man's hand and nodded his acknowledgment.

It was raining the next time he woke. *'I am.'*

He'd been dreaming. He could smell the gum trees in the air. Kate and her girls, his precious daughter … how long had he been asleep?

The Codfish was no longer sitting on the reef. An enemy destroyer was anchored outside the reef and boats were rowing into the shore.

He was the commanding officer. His clothes were dirty and smelly, yet he tried to straighten up his uniform. It was covered in his blood. His men helped him to his feet. They stood together and watched as the boats' officer in charge berated the boy in command of their captors. He struck the boy with his fist, and the boy fell to the sand. Then they approached him and his men.

Name, rank and serial number, that was all he would say. It did not matter how many times they hit him.

It was dark and damp the next time he woke. The dulling of his pain was gone, the morphine was gone. They were in the hull of a vessel. He was arguing with Kate; she wouldn't let him close his eyes. He was tired and didn't know how much longer he could stay.

Heavy boots came down into the hull. A torch was shone around, stirring his men from their sleep. Their bodies and faces battered and bruised, they helped each other up then helped him to his feet. He couldn't do anything as they struggled up the steps with him. On the deck, they were shoved into a lifeboat and rowed to a small sandy island.

He leant on his men as they sat on the shore and watched the boat row back to the ship. Someone tossed a bag over the side of the boat. He saw the face of the boy – he was one of their captors. 'Chief' Morgan waded out to sea and picked up the bag. Rice, matches, some water and a knife.

Maybe enough to keep his men alive.

'I will, Kate.'

He kept his eyes open.

Chapter Thirty-eight

Fremantle, Western Australia.
October 1945

Kate Kelly sat on the front step of her home. She was in her thirty-fourth week of her pregnancy, and it was the first day of October. The midday sun burned her face, and she felt hot. Her neat and tidy garden had taken a lot of time; it filled her days. She'd replanted the lawn and made a flower bed for the rose bush in the centre. It was beginning to show signs of flowering, but the new bush over Sam's grave would not. The one single bud remained closed.

She had visited the specialist, and he was making arrangements for the delivery of her baby. Her mother and sisters had insisted on her accompanying them, and they had shopped for bedding and a layette for the baby. The war had been over nearly seven weeks. The dreams that assaulted her in August and September had left her.

A shadow fell across the land as white tuffs of clouds ran across the blue sky, and a chill ran through Kate. She went to retrieve her cardigan from the front gate. That was when she saw him ... walking slowly up the hilly road. She went to meet him.

His face told her what she already knew. She didn't want to hear the words. 'No, please, no,' she cried and hurried away from him.

He caught up to her as she fumbled with the simple latch on the gate. 'Stupid thing,' she muttered. 'Stupid thing.'

Frank Kelly took her hands and opened the gate. She pulled away from him and stumbled down the pathway to the front step.

'Kate,' he said as he slowly followed her.

She clung to the veranda post, where he placed his hands on her shoulders.

'Don't,' she cried. 'Don't touch me.'

He took a firmer grip on her arms and turned her to face him. She stared at him, her eyes not wanting to see; she didn't want to know.

'Please let me go,' she said.

He did as asked and she held herself straight and tall and walked passed him. Kate returned to the rose bush; knelt in the dirt; picked up her trowel; began turning the soil.

Frank walked down the pathway and stood beside her.

Kate pushed the trowel deep into the dirt. 'What happened?'

'I had a letter from Joe. He wrote it about seven weeks ago. He didn't have much detail, only that the Codfish was lost.'

'With all hands?'

'No. Most of the crew got to safety but ...'

'But?' She plunged the trowel deeper into the dirt.

'Michael was still on board. His crew were in danger, and he managed to protect them long enough to allow their escape. He saved his crew. He is a hero.'

'Another one.'

'You would have expected no less from him.'

'Of course not.'

The trowel dropped from her hands, and she collapsed onto the dirt. When Frank lifted her from the ground, she did not protest. He looked into her eyes.

'You can't do that, Kate,' he said.

'I can, I will.' She would do what she had to.

'It's against God's law,' he said.

'God's law! Why is God's law so hard? How many times do I have to do this?'

'Kate ...' His hands on her arms were firm.

'You're a priest, Frank. You've seen it all before. There has to be a time of peace, a place where there is no more pain and grief. I can't ...'

'Kate ...' He shook her gently.

'No more, Frank, no more.'

She stared at him, and he shook her again.

'What about Jessie? You can't, Kate.'

'Jessie, my little girl.' Her body trembled; the emptiness left her. The calmness evaporated.

'Michael's baby?' Frank said.

Her defences crumbled, and she fought with him, screaming, 'Why? So I can love him; so he can grow up; so he can be sent to fight in a war far away from us ... so he can die in that war?' She stood calmly before him. 'He'd be better off not born.'

'Kate, you don't mean that.'

'Yes I do.'

She pulled herself from his grip; ran past him out the gate and up the hill.

Kate laughed as she stood in front of the monument. The sun was behind grey clouds that had come in over the ocean. Rain fell – large, heavy, warm drops. She saw people scurry about trying to get out of the rain. She cupped her hands together and collected the liquid, startled at the blood-red colour in her palms. When she opened them only rain fell onto the ground.

'Disgusting ... with a bloody Yankee sailor.'

She watched the women walk past.

Men seated at the bar turned to stare as the door opened and the storm outside blew into the warm room. The man behind the bar called his boss.

'Come on, my dear.' Amanda Collins took Kate's arm and sat her beside the fire in the lounge. Kate's cotton smock was wet; her tangled hair fell across her face.

Kate looked around. *Joseph Daniels sat reading at the table near the window. Michael Brannigan stood at the top of the stairs grinning, reaching out to her.*

'Michael ...' Kate stood.

'Sit down, dear.'

'No.'

She shook away the hand that restrained her, and turned to the empty staircase.

Amanda sat Kate down and put a glass to her lips, the liquid burned her throat.

'He's dead. Michael's dead.'

'I'm sorry,' Amanda said. 'I think we'd better get you home.'

The final rays of the setting sun broke through the black storm clouds. Lightning flashed; thunder roared. Rain began to fall, extinguishing the last of the light. The steps of the Pier Hotel were getting wet.

'Tell me where you live. Your baby needs you now,' Amanda said.

The storm within Kate raged. 'I need Michael,' Kate said. She pushed away from the woman and ran into the violent storm.

Kate ignored the discomfort of her pregnancy. She stumbled and fell but kept running until she reached the railway line. Then she walked across the line to the sandy beach, her desperation like the storm raging about her, she fell to her knees and rocked back and forth, keening.

Rain slapped her face. In the lightning, she saw the rough seas pound the shore. The sea … where she always found comfort and joy … the sea that had taken Michael … the sea that would now give her peace.

The anger in the storm still lingered. Stars glittered as they peeked out from behind the rolling clouds that raced inland. Rough seas still pounded the shore.

A light fell across the body on the sand. Frank Kelly placed a lantern on the wet sand and pushed tangled hair away. He helped her sit and wrapped his cloak around her.

'Tell the others we have found her,' Frank said to the young boy who guided him.

*∗∗

Kate stared at the ocean. She had sought peace there, a peace she could not have. She had known that all along; she had to be strong; she was needed.

Frank Kelly lowered himself and sat beside her. Her unborn child moved, and she said, 'I never told Michael. I wish he knew. Do you think he knows now?' She turned to look at him. 'Do you think he knows?'

'Yes. He knows, Kate, that's why he needs you to be strong, for his child and for Jessie, who he loves like his own. He needs you to be strong.'

'I know that.'

She leant into his body and let herself cry … just for a little while, then she would be strong.

Lanterns on the beach approached, voices called out. Frank called back. He picked his cloak up of the sand and wrapped it around her shoulders. She pushed it away, 'I'm hot.'

'No, you're not, you have a fever.' He held the cloak tightly around her and helped her stand.

Kate fell against Frank as pain raced through her. The fluid her unborn child lived in left her body, her legs failed, and she cried out.

'Kate!' Frank said.

'It's the baby.'

The pain of childbirth increased. Kate gasped for breath as it reached its peak, then she slowly regained control of her body as the pain subsided.

'It's too soon. Too soon.'

She clutched his arm as the memory of Jessie's birth – the memory she had tried to forget, pretended hadn't happened – surged into her mind. How hard it had been and how much fear she had for her unborn baby and herself. The doctor finally pulling her beautiful baby girl from her with metal instruments – the bleeding and the pain but mostly the fear for her unborn child. Now she saw the doctor she was attending sitting across from her at his desk, glasses on his nose, balding head, his face grave, his stern voice telling her, 'You must not go into labour. The only way this baby will survive is if it is delivered by caesarean.'

Another contraction. Too soon, too close, intense and painful. Kate doubled over, tried to ease the pain. Sweat poured from her.

'What have I done? What have I done?'

She pleaded with him, 'Frank, my baby must live. Promise me. My baby must live.'

She struggled with the words as this contraction reached its peak. The pain began to subside as the men with the lanterns reached them.

'Kate!' Sean O'Brien called. Another contraction raced through her body, and she fell into her father's arms.

Chapter Thirty-nine

Pearl Harbour, USA. August 1945

Ellen Brannigan, a tall, slim woman in her early sixties, wore her dark silver-streaked hair curled and sitting on the collar of her beige Chanel suit.

On the 8th of August, she received a cable advising her Michael Brannigan was missing, presumed dead. She told her granddaughter that her father was missing. Karen was quiet but not worried. A week later, Ellen received another cable telling her Michael was alive but injured. She had used all her influence and made many calls to her friends. It was almost a week before she had the necessary permits and travel documents for herself and Karen to travel to Pearl Harbour.

On Saturday, 25th August, she sat in a hospital consulting room, waiting. The door opened and a young man in white entered apologising for keeping her waiting. He introduced himself as Doctor Nicholas Jones, shook her hand and sat opposite her at the desk.

'My son … what has happened to him?' Ellen asked.

'He is lucky to be alive.'

'Yes.' She tried to conceal her impatience. A knock on the door agitated her.

'Ah, Chief,' Nicholas Jones said.

She turned to see a thin, red-haired man pushed into the room in a wheelchair.

'This is Mrs Brannigan,' Nicholas said. 'Mrs Brannigan, this is Jack Morgan, from the Codfish.'

Ellen took the hand extended and insisted the man in the wheelchair did not attempt to rise to greet her. Dr Jones continued,

'I think the 'Chief' might be able to give you a better idea about what has happened.'

There are some things a mother shouldn't know, and Ellen understood Jack Morgan was telling her a story. Then he said, 'We didn't know the Captain was injured, ma'am. We would never have left him if we had.'

'You had to follow his orders, 'Chief',' she said.

'Yes, ma'am.'

Jack Morgan turned his eyes away from her. She took his once strong hands and waited for him to continue. 'We ran out of morphine days before we were rescued. I don't know how the Captain stayed alive; maybe it would have been kinder if he hadn't."

'No, never.' Ellen squeezed his hand. 'Never, 'Chief'.'

He continued: 'He should have died, ma'am. I think it was only Mrs Kelly's will that kept him alive.'

'Mrs Kelly?'

'His lady, ma'am.'

'Yes?'

'I know it sounds stupid, but it was as if she was there with him. He would argue with her and talk to her; maybe it was just the fever.'

Ellen could see the man in the wheelchair was beginning to repair from the physical and emotional trauma he had suffered.

She said, 'Thank you, 'Chief'. Without you, my son would not have survived.'

She could see her words had confused him. 'He is alive … that is what matters.'

Ellen turned to Nicholas Jones. 'What injuries does my son have?'

Nicholas Jones said, 'His condition is serious. We had to operate to remove shrapnel from his spine, but his heart stopped beating. We kept him alive but had to leave the remaining shrapnel in his body. We could try again when he is stronger, but it is a great risk, and it might not work.'

'What might not work?'

'He can't move his legs, ma'am, the shrapnel …'

'Not you too,' Ellen whispered.

'Pardon, ma'am?'

'Nothing. Is there anything that can be done?'

'I don't know, ma'am. He is weak, and he has taken such a beating. Removing the rest of the shrapnel might help, but it is dangerous. The arrival of yourself and his daughter should help.'

'His lady, ma'am,' Jack Morgan interrupted. 'He loves her so much … if you had seen him after they met.'

'Yes …' Ellen remembered the letter she had received.

A knock on the door stopped the conversation.

'Come in,' Nicholas Jones answered.

A nurse entered the room and asked if the Chief could be taken back to his bed.

'Thank you, 'Chief',' Ellen said, 'and Mr McDougal … I must see him.'

'He went home … to the mainland, with his parents this morning, ma'am,' Jack Morgan said.

'Was he recovered?'

'Yes, like me. They make a fuss here, pushing people around. I'm sure they've got better things to do.' He gave the nurse a sheepish grin.

'Are you going home soon?'

'Tomorrow. I'm stationed here, and I have my home here. I hope Captain Brannigan recovers.'

Ellen walked through a hospital ward with beds on either side; she saw for the first time what the war had done. Every bed occupied, bodies and minds scarred and mutilated. She understood Michael's objection to her making money out of a military contract. Boots for men to die in, profiteering from the war, he had said. He always was more of a sailor than a warrior. She vowed not one cent from that contact would remain with her family.

At the end of the ward, behind a drawn curtain, Michael Brannigan fought for his life. She thought she had prepared herself, but this thin, battered man was her son – her little boy lying helpless and injured. She had always been strong – kept her emotions close, but it was her son who struggled for life, just like his father. Nicholas Jones helped her to chair beside the bed.

'Michael,' she whispered, then turned to the doctor and asked, 'Can he hear me?'

'Sometimes.'

'Michael,' she spoke louder. 'Come on, Michael, you can do this.'

'I can't.'

He could barely speak through cracked lips. Ellen dampened her fingers in the glass on the bedside table and wet his lips.

'Yes, you can,' she said firmly.

'I can't, Kate. I'm tired.'

It hurt that he didn't know who she was, but she took his hand and talked to him.

'You must, Michael. Karen needs you. I need you. We have waited too long for you to come home. You can't leave us now.'

'Mum.'

Mum? She would take any acknowledgment.

'Yes, Michael.'

He had opened his eyes. 'Mother,' he said, 'where's Karen?' She could see the pain the words caused him. She could see how hard it was for him to talk, but he was coming back to her.

'With Beth.'

'Good,' he said and closed his eyes.

'Michael!'

'Let him rest now,' Nicholas Jones said. 'Come back tomorrow.'

Ellen returned the next day with her granddaughter. She had told Karen exactly what to expect. Ellen had bought her up the best she could since her mother died and her father had gone to war. They were alike in many ways and, as she had grown older, her stoic nature began to appear. Now she was a frightened little girl clinging to the hand of a man she had been told was her father.

***

Karen Brannigan remembered Daddy as being big and strong. This poor man was so thin and so sick. He looked a bit like Daddy –if he opened his eyes she might know – it was a long time since she'd seen him. She didn't want to cry.

'It's all right, Karen,' her grandmother said.

'Don't die, Daddy. Please don't die,' she said.

'I won't die, Poppet.'

His words were so quiet she could hardly hear them, but she had heard one word. *Poppet.* No-one called her Poppet, except Daddy. It really was him. He was home.

'Daddy,' Karen wept.

She sat on the bed, closer to him and leant her head on his chest. He closed his arms around her.

Her Daddy was home. She had been a good girl for Grandmother. She missed Mummy and Jamie. Grandmother had said she must work hard and pray for Daddy so he would be safe, and she had.

He was home instead of only having his letters and the funny presents he used to send, each one so precious even though they never fitted, and were too childish for her. This year when he sent presents, they were the right size and suitable for her; she had wondered about that.

'Let me see you.' He was talking.

She sat up so he could see her.

***

Michael Brannigan saw his daughter through eyes blurred by tears, pain and drugs. 'How beautiful you are.'

His eyes would not stay open, no matter how hard he tried. Wandering through his mind, another girl a little older, with red hair … what had happened to her father? He drifted on a sea of pain and drugs and heard a voice say, *Will you be my daddy?*

'Yes, Jessie,' he forced the words out of his dazed mind.

'Daddy! Daddy!' he heard his daughter scream. He tried to open his eyes.

He heard: 'It's okay, little one. He is tired and needs to sleep. Let him rest now.'

***

Ellen kissed her son's forehead.

'Come on, Karen. We will see him tomorrow.'

She took her granddaughter's hand, and they walked through the hospital ward.

'Who is Jessie, Grandmother?' Karen asked.

'I don't know,' Ellen lied.

Chapter Forty

Michael Brannigan began to recover. The number of drugs necessary to keep him out of pain was reduced. Good food and kind attention allowed his body to repair. He looked forward to the visit from his mother and daughter.

'Where is Karen?' Michael asked as his mother sat beside his bed.

'It's a lovely day; she has gone to the beach with Beth and the boys.'

He knew what she wanted to talk about, and he turned his head to look out the window. The sun shone in a clear blue sky, bright coloured hibiscus trees bloomed in the gardens. How was he going to do this? He had too. He turned to face his mother.

'Michael, I have spoken to Henry. I can get permits for Kate and the girls to travel immediately,' Ellen said.

'No,' he said.

'Michael?'

He sat up straight and said, 'I won't ask her …'

He hadn't talked to his mother about Kate, he couldn't get the words to come out. Sometime in his sleep, he would talk to Kate and sometimes when he woke his mother was sitting listening to him. Just the mention of Kate's name was tearing him to pieces. He had to be strong. He took a deep breath and regained control.

'Don't you want her to come?' his mother asked.

How could she say that? He couldn't speak, his throat was tight, of all the pain he'd suffered, nothing hurt him like this. The plans he'd made, the life they were going to share. He had to love her enough; he had to be strong.

'Don't you think she will come?' Ellen asked.

'Of course, she will come. I will not have her waste her life with a cripple. I don't want her too …'

He looked at his mother and said slowly and deliberately, 'I saw you, Mother. I saw you live with Father; how hard it was. I saw you cry when you thought no one was around. When he died, I heard them, the Aunts and Uncles, I heard them at his funeral. 'It was a blessing, for the best, a release for Ellen'; you never cried then.'

'Not in public, Michael, but I cried.' She took his hand. 'I loved your father; he gave up so much for the love we shared. Did you never think, Michael … did you never think why your life was so different from your cousins? Why you didn't have the same religious upbringing as them? We loved each other so much. If I could have had one more day with him, I would have. I didn't care how hard it was, but he suffered; he was in pain. When he died, I cried. You should have asked me, not listened to the silly gaggle.'

'I'm sorry.'

He had thought about that – he had no religious upbringing. He wondered why, but as a child and young man, the love he had received from his parents was all he needed. When Carol had wanted to christen their children, he had no objections. And he found out that his mother's religion, the one she had not practised for all her married life, was the one his children belonged to.

'Look at me, Michael. I don't believe you can love like you do without that love being returned. It's fate or something. I don't know.'

'Maybe … when I have the next operation.'

'No, Michael, you can't; it's too dangerous. At least write to Kate.'

His resolve faltered.

'No.' He had to be strong.

'Don't be stupid, Michael. How can you be so selfish?'

'Selfish?'

'Yes, Michael.'

She fumbled in her bag.

'Here …' She thrust an envelope into his hands. '… read this and tell me you're not being selfish.'

Michael watched his mother's back as she walked down the ward. He opened the letter and a small photograph fell onto his lap. Kate and Jessie smiled up at him. He read his letter.

Dear Mother,

Today I have wonderful news, for today I have asked my darling Kate to marry me, and she has said yes.

I met Kate just before Christmas and have spent much of this last leave with her. She lost her husband in the war, she has a daughter Jessie who is six and her niece Tilly who is fourteen is also in her care. I have not told Karen. I don't want to write it in a letter. I'm sure Kate will love her as I love Jessie. But Karen will need time. I hope the war will end soon and we can all come home.

I cannot explain my feeling for Kate. She takes my breath away, she has given me hope. I can remember Carol and share those memories with Karen, and I can now think about my little boy. Without Kate I don't think I would be able to do this. Neither of us thought we would fall in love again, but it's as if our lives have become bound together. I know that doesn't make much sense and I ask your forgiveness for my silly boyish prattle.

I am well.

Your loving son.

Michael.

The last words blurred. *What am I doing?*

Michael Brannigan was writing letters. He had spent the last few days arguing with Nicholas Jones, and now he was making sure he had done all he needed.

He had written to Kate telling her he was injured and having surgery. He told her that, when he recovered, he would come and get her and Jessie and bring them home, telling her he hoped this would be very soon. All of this, he wanted to happen. He had posted that letter.

He had written to his daughter telling her how happy he was to have seen her, and what a beautiful girl she was, how he wished he could have seen her grow up and how he wanted her to be happy. He told her he loved her and hoped she would understand when she was older. He had put that letter in an envelope with a note for his mother.

Now he told Kate the truth. He told her his body was crippled. He would not let her spend her life looking after that body. He was having surgery to make sure that wouldn't happen. That surgery was dangerous, and he might not survive it. He saw her standing before him telling him it was not his choice to make, that she could and would look after him no matter how damaged his body was. He knew she would do that, but he could not allow it, he loved her too much for that. He told her he loved her and would love her forever, no matter where he was. He couldn't tell her to move on with her life. He couldn't write those words on the paper, there had to be some hope he would survive.

She wouldn't understand why he had done this, but in time he hoped she would forgive him.

He sealed this letter as Nicholas Jones came into the room and said, 'We are ready.'

✳✳✳

Ellen Brannigan stood facing an empty bed, trying to keep calm. Nicholas Jones called her name. She turned slowly, deliberately, stood tall and straight.

'He is out of surgery,' Nicholas said.

'What surgery? Did he become ill?'

'Didn't you know?'

'What?' She kept calm.

'Let's sit down.'

She sat on the chair by the bed; he sat on the bed.

'Your son has had the additional surgery to remove the remaining shrapnel from his spine. He is in a serious but stable condition.'

'Why? Why did you do this when you knew it might kill him?'

'He knew all the risks. I tried to talk him out of it, but he was determined, threatening to leave the hospital.'

'Oh my God,' Ellen covered her mouth with her hands.

Nicholas Jones said, 'He's a fighter, ma'am. To stay alive so far I am hopeful he will recover. He asked me to give you these.'

He handed her two envelopes.

'Can I see him?'

'No, not yet. He is in intensive care. I will get in touch with you if there is any change.'

Ellen sat on a bench under a shady tree and opened the letter addressed to her.

It read.

> *Dear Mother,*
>
> *Forgive me for not discussing this with you. I will not ask Kate to come to me as I am, and you are right, I cannot leave her without any word from me. I have written to her telling her I am alive and having surgery. The letter you have is for Kate if I do not recover. Please read the letter I have written to Karen and see that she understands when you give it to her. I know you will look after her. Tell her I love her.*
>
> *Please forgive me, I am a selfish coward.*
>
> *I love you.*
>
> *Michael.*

Ellen Brannigan wept. 'You stupid, stupid boy.'

Three-week later Ellen Brannigan stood in the doorway watching her son on the lawn. His body was filling out; repairing itself. Exercise strengthened his limbs, but he was still confined to a wheelchair. She watched him force himself out of that chair, take his weight on his legs and fall to the ground. She saw him pull himself back into his chair, pound his fists into his legs and try again.

'Ellen.'

'Thank goodness you're here.'

Joseph Daniels held her gently and kissed her on the cheek.

'How is Michael?' Joe looked past her to Michael on the lawn.

'Joe, I don't know what to do with him. He won't come home.

I can get nurses, a doctor, but he refuses, saying he will go to a hostel.'

She saw her son in the wheelchair, trying, forcing himself and failing.

'Three days ago, when I came to see him, he said he had to go to Australia, just like that. He hasn't mentioned Kate's name since the operation, now he's insisting on travelling to see her. We argued the doctors said he should wait longer before attempting such a journey, but he won't listen. I received this today.' She handed him a brown window-faced envelope.

'Maybe he knew. I'm afraid of what it will do to him.'

Joe Daniels took the cable and read.

> *Kate unable to travel.*
> *Seriously ill after childbirth.*
> *Baby struggling to survive.*

It was signed Sean O'Brien.

'Michael's baby?' Ellen asked.

'Yes.'

'God damn it,' Joe cursed, then he remembered his manners and apologised to her.

'Kate would have come, Michael knows that. She thinks he's lost at sea. I had to write that letter. I thought he would write to her,' Joe said.

'He did write to her before the operation,' Ellen said. 'But I had already sent her a letter … against his wishes. I asked her to come, I told her what had happened. I felt sure she would come. I didn't know about the baby, Michael never said anything.'

'He doesn't know,' Joe said.

Ellen straightened her skirt and said, 'How stupid we've all been. I'd better show him.'

'May I? I would like to talk to him,' Joe said.

Ellen watched Joe walk across the green lawn. He called out Michael's name as he approached. She saw the pleasure on her son's face at seeing his friend. As Joe and Michael talked angry words and

raised voices were blown away by the wind. She saw her son
desperately trying to get out of the chair that bound him. He pushed
Joe's hand away and fell to the lawn; he let his friend help him up.
She watched as he read the cable and saw despair take the fight out
of him; his head slumped to his chest. She saw him sit up straight.
Ellen walked across the lawn and stood beside his chair.

'It is time to go,' Michael Brannigan said.

Chapter Forty-one

Fremantle, Western Australia.
October 1945

Kathleen O'Brien stood on the dock in Fremantle. It was October 3rd, 1945. The ship her son travelled on had finally docked. He had been in a prison camp for over three years. It had taken nearly seven weeks to arrange his passage home.

Matilda stood beside her holding her grandfather's hand. She knew her father would look different, that he had been very sick and treated cruelly and that he hadn't had much to eat for a long time. What else could she tell a fifteen-year-old girl?

Kathleen heard her son call out as he walked down the gangway. He was thin, his face covered in scars; he had lost teeth, and his hair was grey and sparce.

Matilda hesitated. He was nothing like the man she remembered. He called her name again, and she ran into his arms as he came off the gangway.

'Let me see you,' Robert said. He pushed her gently away. 'My little girl,' he said. 'You have grown.'

He ran his hands through her ringlets. 'Look at you. Such a beautiful young woman. You look just like your mother.'

She could see tears in his eyes. Matilda cried.

Kathleen wanted to hold her son, but she knew how long Tilly had waited for this; how brave she had been all this time. She would wait.

Matilda took her hand and put her in the arms of the boy she had waited so long to see. Sean stood back, as always, then he stepped forward and took their son in his arms and held him tight.

They pushed their way through the crowds on the dock. Robert asked, 'Where's Kate?'

Kathleen sat with Robert as he held the hand of his dying sister.

'Isn't there anything you can do?' Robert asked Joshua Fredericks, who stood taking Kate's pulse.

'It's been three days now,' Joshua said. 'If it hadn't been such an emergency …

'It was a complicated delivery. I couldn't wait any longer for the specialist – I would have lost them both. She was fighting me all the way. I couldn't calm her; she kept telling me I must save her baby. She was fighting the nurse. Then she calmed and whispered something. All she wanted me to do was save her baby. We finally got her sedated, there was nothing I could do but operate, the baby struggled for life. I did what I could.'

'We know you did,' Kathleen said. 'Kate had some terrible news that day. I'm not sure if she wants to stay with us anymore. We will just have to wait and pray.'

'No,' Robert growled. 'We can't just sit here. I've seen too much of this. She can't die. Look at all this medicine, it's clean, it's sterile, it wasn't like this in Changi.' He choked. 'No-one should die with all this.'

Kathleen put her arm around her son's shoulder.

Robert shook Kate gently. 'Come on, Katey, you've got to try, you know you can.'

'This came for Kate,' Sean O'Brien said as he came into the room.

Robert took the envelope, opened it and read the letter. Then he read aloud to his sister.

5th September 1945

My dear Kate,

I presume upon your love for Michael when I write this. He has come back to us, his body battered and broken, almost beyond repair, his mind dazed, and his spirit disoriented.

He has suffered serious injuries. The doctors are hopeful of his

'Michael's alive, Kate. Did you hear? … he's alive, and he needs you. Come on, Kate,' Robert shook her shoulder.

Kathleen placed a restraining hand on his arm, but he shrugged it off. 'Come on! Remember, you're an O'Brien and 'we're tough', remember.'

Kate didn't move, her dirty, dull hair was tied to one side, her breathing slow and shallow. 'I'm tough,' she mumbled.

'Yes, Kate, you're tough,' Robert said. He took Kate's hand. 'You can do it, come on.'

***

Kate was falling. She couldn't move; couldn't escape. Michael was dead. Jessie, the baby, what had happened? Too much pain, too much grief, she couldn't do this alone, not again.

'No,' she slipped back into unconsciousness, where there was no pain, no grief.

Chapter Forty-two

Kate Kelly opened the gate. It was such a long time since she had felt so peaceful. She walked down the path; he rose from the front step to meet her, a black and white Kelpie puppy in his arms. The sunny, windless day showed the garden at its best.

'I thought I told you to be careful.' Kate shook her head.

'I know,' he said.

'You never did much I asked, did you?'

'Not much. Sometimes you gotta do what you gotta do.' A grin spread across his face.

'I know. Do you understand?'

'Your happiness is dear to me.'

'And?'

'We both understand.'

'You're a good man.'

'Always. Can't stay, though; gotta go.'

'I'll come with you.'

'You can't. You have to look after the children.'

Sunshine faded in the garden, and the wind blew dry leaves past her feet.

'The baby?' Kate asked.

'He needs you.'

'Michael.'

Dust flew into her face, and thunder roared.

'Let me come with you?' she pleaded.

'You can't, Kate.'

'Please … I must find Michael. Help me?'

'I can't. You have to stay with the children.'

Rain slashed her face with dirt and grit. Thunder roared. And the garden shook.

'I'll go back. I know I have too. Please just let me say goodbye to Michael. I'll go back.'

The wind began to subside.

'You can't go back if you come with me.'

He walked past her, the puppy at his heels. He opened the gate to leave the garden.

'Patrick!' she cried.

'Goodbye, my darling.' He hesitated, his hand on the gate and said, 'Michael's not here.'

'Goodbye, Patrick,' she said.

The storm vanished.

Kate surrendered. She was not alone.

'Michael's alive,' she said.

Kate heard a voice.

'He's alive, Kate.'

'Bobby?' Her eyes were barely open. Was it really him?

Her brother took her hand and held it to his lips. 'Yes,' he said.

'My baby? My baby?' Kate tried to sit, but the pain forced her into her brother's arms. 'Bobby, my baby?'

'A boy,' Joshua Fredericks said as he came into the room.

'Is he all right? Can I see him?'

'He's alive. He's been in the humidity crib … he's a tough little fighter.'

'Can I see him? Jessie? Where's Jessie?'

'She's with Mary Kelly.' Robert lay her gently on the pillow. Kate closed her eyes.

'Kate.' She heard her mother's voice.

'It's all right,' Joshua Fredericks said. 'Let her rest. I'll get the baby.'

Joshua Fredericks returned to the room, a small bundle in his arms.

'Kate.'

She opened her eyes, and he placed the child in her arms. 'Here, he is.'

All Kate could see was the top of her child's head. She forced herself to sit and look into his face.

'Hello.' She kissed the top of his head, breathing him in. 'He's so small.'

'Yes, but he is tough,' the doctor said.

'He's an O'Brien,' her brother said.

'Yes,' she replied.

Kate was in a white room. Her parents and Bobby, her big brother, sat beside her bed, Frank Kelly by her side where she knew he would be.

Frank said, 'I named him Michael.'

She remembered him by her bed; she remembered him blessing her with oil. 'That is right,' Kate replied.

Kate's eyes began to close. She felt her mother take her child from her arms. 'Jessie? Jessie, is she all right?'

Had she seen her daughter crying, somewhere nearby – was it real or just a dream?

Her mother said, 'She's all right, Kate. We left her with Mary today as she got upset last time we brought her to see you. But we will be able to bring her back now.'

Kate's eyes opened in alarm. 'Michael, he's hurt; he needs me.' She tried to move but could not make her body obey her thoughts. She couldn't get out of the bed.

'You are going nowhere, my girl,' Joshua Fredericks said. 'If you don't stay in this bed and get better, you will be of no use to anyone, not Michael, not his child, Jessie or yourself.'

Kate closed her eyes and her ears to the scolding. She would sleep, dream, then she would get out of this bed.

The next ten days were intolerable for Kate, the slow process of recovering taking its time. She always did what she was told; was always bright and happy, never getting out of bed; she was a good patient. She began to feel fit and healthy. Her little baby began to thrive. She was able to feed him, hold and love him, but was not allowed to do any more for him.

Kate asked if she could get out of her bed, but Joshua Fredericks would have none of it, so she continued to be a good patient. Her family kept the chair by her bed occupied during the day. The only time she was alone was at night, and she began trying to get out of bed, but the pain would force her back in tears.

Two weeks after her baby was born, Kate was allowed out of bed, but only under strict supervision. She was allowed to bathe her baby and walked a few steps around the ward. She smiled and hid the pain this caused her. When Jessie came to see her, she put the roses from the garden in the vase. And under medical supervision, she was allowed to sit in the sunshine in the garden.

Kate pleaded with Peg to send a telegram to Ellen Brannigan asking her to arrange documents and fares for her and the children. Peg relented but only on the promise that Kate would not attempt such a journey without the doctor's permission. Kate was surprised at how easily she lied to her friend.

As this week came to an end, Kate's need to be with Michael became obsessive. She was dreaming again – he was in pain – she needed to get out of this hospital. Night was the only time she was alone; she must make Joshua realise she was well enough to leave the hospital. She would show him in the morning that she could walk unaided and then she would go home. He could not stop her.

She sat in the bed and forced her legs over the side onto the floor and stood. She let go of the bed; she was going to get out of this place; she would prove to him that it was time to let her go. One step at a time, that was all it would take. One step at a time. It was harder than she thought, harder than she remembered. It should be easy, one foot after the other. Why was it so hard?

Her legs crumbled under her. She reached for a chair, but it moved with her, and she fell. She couldn't move. The floor was sticky under her – that wasn't right – hospital floors should be clean. She could no longer make out objects in the room.

Chapter Forty-three

Jessica Kelly pushed her grandfather away and ran from the room, crying. Everything was good, Mummy was getting better, and baby Michael was lovely. Mummy would let her hold him, and soon they were going to bring him home, then they were going to see 'Tenant Michael. Mummy said he was too sick to come and see them, so they would be going on a big adventure to see him. She wasn't a baby anymore – she was a big sister now – she was seven, and she missed him. Harry's daddy had come home, and so had Uncle Robert, and she wanted 'Tenant Michael to be her daddy.

She had gone to pick the rose from where they had put Sam, but it was on the ground, and that made her sad. She had brushed the dirt off it. It still looked pretty so she had put it in a glass of water to bring to Mummy. When Nannie and Poppy bought her to see Mummy. She looked white, and there was a tube in her arm, and that tube had red stuff in it. Dr Fredericks was in the room. Baby Michael was in the crib, not in Mummy's arms and Uncle Frank was there. Dr Fredericks spoke to Nannie and Poppy, and no one spoke to her.

Mummy couldn't hold the rose – her hands were shaking. Poppy had given her a letter from 'Tenant Michael. That should have made Mummy happy, but Mummy cried and tried to get out of bed. Jessie was scared; she did not want to stay in that room. She stumbled into the corridor, her eyes full of tears, and she did not see the other people there until she collided with them. Jessie looked at the man. He lifted her onto his knees, and she wrapped her arms around his neck as he held her.

***

Michael Brannigan held the little girl to his heart. He had made the long journey with his mother's help: it had taken almost three weeks. He still couldn't walk, but he forced himself out of the wheelchair every night. He would not let his mother attend to his personal needs. If there was pain, he ignored it: he had to keep going; he had to get home. His family needed him.

When they landed in Brisbane almost a week ago, he could smell the eucalyptus in the air. Kate loved the green trees and the blue sky, and he took strength from that to continue his journey. He had left his precious daughter in the care of his trusted friend, with a promised he would be back soon. He would keep that promise.

Sean O'Brien came into the hallway and took Jessie out of his arms.

Michael could hear a raised voice coming from the room Jessie had run out of. He pushed his wheelchair as hard as he could; stopped at the doorway of the hospital room.

'Kate,' he called.

She didn't hear him.

Kate pushed at the hands that were trying to help her. He could see his letter in her hands – she cradled it to her like a baby. She shouldn't be so distressed by it. She stopped struggling and lay in the bed muttering. 'No. No.'

'Kate,' he called again.

His mother rushed to the bed, sat and took Kate by the shoulders. 'Kate,' Ellen said. 'Kate, listen to me. Michael survived the operation. He survived.'

Kate opened her eyes.

'He survived,' Ellen repeated.

Kate closed her eyes. Her face became calm, and her body went limp. His letter fell to the floor.

'No,' Michael howled.

The fear he had felt that summer's day surrounded him as he looked at her lifeless body.

'No …'

He stumbled across the room; collapsed into strong hands that sat him on the bed before they took Kate's wrist. Frank Kelly kissed his purple sash and began to pray.

'No, not now. Not now,' he begged.

He lowered his forehead to hers. His eyes were dim, and the voices in the room echoed far away from him. How could he have been so stupid to think she could live without him? He'd been selfish and cruel. He could not bear to live without her, but he knew he had too. He had made promises to two little girls, and he would keep those promises.

He wept. 'I'm sorry. I'm sorry.'

The fingers on his cheeks were cold – they wiped his tears away. He lifted his head. Kate was looking at him.

'I'm sorry,' he said.

'Hush, hush,' she replied.

She tried to sit, and he lifted her gently and held her to him. She folded herself inside his embrace.

Kate was in his arms; it was so long since he'd held her. He remembered her scent, the way she curled her hands together when she folded into his arms, the way she fitted into him.

***

Kate was in Michael's arms. It was so long since she'd been in his arms. She remembered everything – his touch – his scent – the beat of his heart.

She had fought to keep him alive, to keep herself alive. She was tired. She gathered strength in his embrace, pulled herself a little tighter and lay her head on his chest to hear his heartbeat, to be close to him, to be part of him.

The baby cried.

The child's grandmother took him from the crib.

'There is someone who wants to meet you,' Kathleen O'Brien said.

Michael lay Kate gently back on the pillow, then he took the child in his arms.

'Our little boy,' Kate said.

'I should have been here,' he said.

'You didn't know. I was foolish, I'm sorry,' Kate closed her eyes. She heard Michael cry her name.

Kate opened her eyes 'It wasn't a dream. You are here?' she whispered.

'I am here,' he replied. 'I will be here forever.'

'Forever.'

Laying the child on the bed beside her, he took Kate's face in his hands and caressed her lips. She could not keep her eyes open as she returned his kisses, as she sought his touch.

Michael picked their baby up, placed him on her lap and lifted them both gently into his arms.

***

Sean O'Brien stood in the doorway, his granddaughter in his arms, Ellen Brannigan beside him.

'He'll be okay now,' Ellen said.

Jessica Kelly slid to the floor and walked into her daddy's welcoming arms.

Sean said, 'They all will.'

Introduction to the sequel –

Tomorrow's Promise

23rd February 1969
95th Evacuation Hospital
Da Nang, Vietnam.

Dear Captain and Mrs Brannigan,

It is my sad duty to inform you that your son Michael
Francis Brannigan is missing.

Our medical outpost in Da Nang was overrun by the
Vietcong on January 25th. Your son and two other medics
managed to evacuate most of the patients in the unit
before we were overrun. When we were able to return to
the outpost, there was no sign of your son.

His heroic actions against such odds saved many lives.
You can be proud of this.

Your country is forever in your debt.

Major John Alexander Smith.
United States Army, Surgical Service.

About the Author

Bernadette lives in Secret Harbour, Western Australia, and writes from an Australian perspective.

She grew up in country Western Australia, where her father drove wheat trains. Those days were filled with adventures, running barefoot through the bush. Her family moved to the outer suburbs of Perth and she attended school in Victoria Park.

Working as an office assistant, Bernadette saved enough money for another adventure in the 70s, sailing around the world on the grand old Liner Australis, living in London, planting potatoes in Jersey, and learning to ski on a Contiki tour to Australia. After that, she backpacked with a tent and a Eurail train pass.

In 2012, Queen Mary II made her inaugural cruise circumnavigating Australia, and Bernadette joined her. She likes to travel and has seen London, Paris, Berlin and Amsterdam. Then COVID hit. Now she travels around Australia, which is a truly amazing country.

When Bernadette's not being a mum and grand-mum, she spends her time writing. Tomorrow's Roses came from stories told to Bernadette by her mother and her mother's twin sister about how Perth was like a movie set full of American servicemen. Her mother's twin sister met a young man from a submarine. He visited for two weeks and promised to return, leaving a book he treasured in her care. He never returned.

Her father delivered telegrams during the war.